Sentimental Tales

Exploring the stories of Nikolai Karamzin and his influences

Translated and edited by
Helen Hagon

Translation and editorial content copyright 2024 by Helen Hagon

All rights reserved

ISBN: 9798324452537

To Natasha

Thank you for starting it all.

Contents

Introduction 7
Part 1: Julia 13
   Eugene and Julia 15
   Eugénie and Léonce 28
   The Nightingale 45
Part 2: Liza 49
   Poor Liza 52
   The Nosegay 81
   The Stationmaster 84
   Eternal Memory 106
   The Graveyard 107
Part 3: The Stranger in Gravesend 111
   Bornholm Island 113
   Extract from 'A Hero of Our Time' 134
   Clouds 137
   The Shore 138
Part 4: An Unlikely Knight 139
   A Knight of Our Time 141
   Actaeon's Odyssey on Ilkley Moor 186

Forgive Me	190
Epilogue	192
Bibliography	194
Acknowledgements	196
About the translator	197

Introduction

Many years ago, as a student learning Russian, I read and fell in love with Nikolai Karamzin's sentimental tale, *Poor Liza*. It was the first Russian 'novel' I managed to read all by myself (if you can call it a novel at just over 5,000 words), and in addition to feeling a sense of achievement, I also found the melodramatic style resonated with my teenage sensibilities. A few decades later, I returned to my rather faded copy and decided to translate it, just for fun, whilst writing a blog reflecting on the translation process, which I called 'Liza's Journey'. It wasn't long, though, before the project snowballed and grew much bigger than I had imagined, as I started reading more of Karamzin's stories and learning about the Sentimentalist movement and its impact on Russian literature. I found myself falling down a literary rabbit hole, and when I eventually emerged, slightly dazed and rubbing my eyes, this book was the result of my adventures.

Nikolai Mikhailovich Karamzin was born into a noble family in provincial Russia in 1766. He was sent to be educated in Moscow, later moving on to St. Petersburg, and eventually to Simbirsk, meeting other literary figures, translating foreign literature into English, editing journals and writing his own works along the way. In 1789, Karamzin set out on a trip around Europe, visiting Germany, Switzerland, France and England. He kept a detailed journal of his travels, which was published as *Letters of a Russian Traveller* upon his return.

As a result of his education, aptitude for foreign languages, and first-hand experience of life in Western Europe, Karamzin was very well read and had an excellent knowledge of European literature, including Jean-Jacques Rousseau, Laurence Sterne, Salomon Gessner, Virgil, Ovid, and many more. The Sentimentalist movement was in full swing in Europe at that time, and Karamzin's own sentimental tales were a clear attempt to develop a similar style of writing in the Russian language. Russian literature was not as well developed as its Western European counterpart at the time, and Karamzin's attempts to write stories that would appeal to a more general readership, including women and children, were quite unusual, if not trailblazing. His style and language deviated from that of the traditional epic tales, adopting the more personal, emotional approach of the Sentimentalist writers, and laying down the foundations of a vernacular literary language which would then be developed further by the well-known Russian literary greats who followed in Karamzin's wake.

Karamzin was not, of course, the only Russian writer attempting to forge a new kind of Russian literature. He also had the likes of Fyodor Emin, Mikhail Chulkov, and Mikhail Kheraskov, among others, for company. Karamzin's efforts, however, possibly had the most lasting influence.

The third and final phase of Karamzin's writing life was arguably his most serious. With the support and encouragement of the Tsar himself, Alexander I, he spent the rest of his life working on a 12-volume *History of the Russian State*. Although the full work was never finished, as Karamzin died whilst working on volume 11, it was a huge undertaking and is still a highly regarded academic work to this day.

This collection of stories and poems focuses on Karamzin's sentimental tales, and the four parts are named after the main characters in the stories. Each section begins with one of Karamzin's tales, followed by the work of another writer who either influenced, or was influenced by Karamzin, namely Mme de Genlis, Gessner, Pushkin and Lermontov. Separating the various sections are translations of some of Karamzin's poetry. Finally, on a couple of occasions, I gave in to temptation and penned a few verses of my own in response to the stories.

The four stories by Karamzin are arranged in chronological order, according to the date they were written: *Eugene and Julia* (1789), *Poor Liza* (1792),

Bornholm Island (1793) and *A Knight of our Time* (1802-1803). When reading them in this order, the progression of Karamzin's writing style becomes clear, from a saccharine-sweet, idyllic beginning, to deeper character development, the addition of a Gothic element, and eventually a shift towards sarcasm and parody.

All the translations in this book are my own, with one exception. German not being one of my main working languages, I opted to include George Baker's 1809 translation of Gessner's idyll *The Nosegay,* as I think it fits excellently into Liza's chapter.

Karamzin's language is, for the most part, relatively straightforward and not too difficult to translate. However, the aspect which proved the most challenging of all was the punctuation. There is an abundance of long sentences divided by colons, which might feel a little strange to a modern-day English-speaking reader. After much deliberation, instead of splitting them all up, or going the opposite way and leaving them all unaltered, I decided to adopt a combination of both approaches, changing some where I felt the English might flow better, and leaving others which seemed to work as they were.

There were also some specific cultural references and names which raised the question of whether to substitute, simplify, or translate literally. For example, the term 'sazhen' is used a few times as a measure of distance (2.13 metres), and there are several references to the 'svirel', a wooden pipe, similar to a flute or recorder. Again, I have employed a variety of solutions for these – sometimes including a gloss, sometimes adding a footnote, sometimes substituting an English equivalent, and sometimes keeping the original term – depending on how much I thought the reader would be able to infer and understand, and what I felt the flow of the language required most.

This project has been good company for about a year, so now it is complete, what will I do next? Work and family permitting, I am tempted to investigate Karamzin's travel diary more closely, and I feel I may have left things unfinished by not translating some of the other sentimental tales, such as *Sierra Morena* or *My Confession*. Then there must be hundreds of other writers from all periods of history waiting to be explored...

Part 1: Julia

For the first part of their story, Eugene and Julia are living the dream. Everything is perfect, there is sweetness and light in abundance, and no-one is led astray or makes mistakes. Even when things eventually go wrong, no-one is to blame, and everyone must simply accept that it was the will of God. As is typical of the Sentimentalist idyll, nature plays a significant role, with birds, flowers, trees, water and weather reflecting the characters' moods and the action of the story.

As Karamzin's writing style progressed, the narrator became an important element of his stories. Eugene and Julia being one of his earlier works, published in the journal *Detskoye Chiteniya*, or *Children's Reading*, in 1789, the narrator is not quite so apparent, although a cameo appearance at the end of the story by a 'sensitive young man' who visits the village, is possibly the narrator himself.

Karamzin's *Eugene and Julia* is paired here with *Eugénie and Léonce* by Madame de Genlis, a contemporary of Karamzin and a prolific writer on the French literary scene in the late 18th and early 19th century. In addition to their similar titles, the stories have much in common. Like their Russian counterparts, Eugénie and Léonce are flawless characters living a blissful life, and the setting is an integral part of the story, echoing the thoughts and actions of the protagonists. As in the previous story, the potential arises for things to go awry, but the characters' innocence remains intact, and the idyll is rendered even more perfect.

Eugene and Julia
A true Russian story
by Nikolai Mikhailovich Karamzin

Cessez et retenez ces clameurs lamentables
Faible soulagement aux maux des misérables!
Fléchissons sous un Dieu, qui veut nous eprouver,
Qui d'un mot peut nous perdre, et d'un mot nous sauver![1]

(Voltaire, 'Oedipe')

Having spent all her youth in Moscow, Mrs L. eventually moved away to a village and lived there in almost complete isolation, with only her ward for company, the daughter of a late acquaintance who, in the last days of her life, had taken her by the hand and said, 'Be a mother to my Julia!'

Their peaceful life flowed along like a calm, clear river streaming with innocent pleasures and chaste

---

[1]*Cease and refrain from this regrettable lamentation,*
For the misery of the poor such meagre consolation!
Let us bow down to a God who would put us to the test,
Who can smite us with a word, but with another save and bless! (Voltaire, 'Oedipus')

delights. The idleness and boredom which oppress many country people did not dare to go near them. They were always occupied with something; their hearts and minds were always busy. Scarcely would the dark shadows of night begin to dissipate and the rosy light of dawn pervade the air, than Mrs L. would wake with nature, then gently interrupt Julia's peaceful sleep with caresses and invite her to make the most of the morning's loveliness. They would hug each other before leaving the house and sitting high up on a hill to await the sun and greet it with gladness. Having enjoyed this magnificent spectacle of nature, they would return home feeling cheerful, then stroll around the garden and look at the flowers, admiring their fresh beauty and drinking in their ambrosial scents. When Mrs L. spied a luxuriant rose, she would often cast a glance at Julia and smile at the considerable resemblance between the two. Of all the flowers, though, Julia loved violets the most. 'Sweet little flower!' she would say, brushing her lips against its leaves. 'Sweet little flower! You hide among the thick grass in vain: I will find you wherever you are.' As she said this, she vowed to herself that she would always be humble like her beloved violets. After lunch, they would go to watch the villagers working in the fields, and the workers laboured cheerily in their presence. The evening brought more enjoyment. They gazed at the setting sun, and at the gentle sheep running home, bleating and leaping to the sound of the shepherd's pipe, and they watched the work-weary villagers walking, one after another, back to the village. Pleased with their successful day's efforts, the people blessed Mother Nature and their lot in life with simple songs, and the two women listened.

When cloudy autumn set in, covering all of creation with a thick blanket of gloom, or when the harsh winter rushed down from the north and shook the world with its storms, it was then that a languid melancholy crept into Julia's gentle heart, and her chest was racked with soft sighs. At that point they would turn to books; the immortal creations of true philosophers who wrote for the benefit of the human race. They would also read and re-read letters from their dear Eugene, Mrs L.'s son who was studying abroad. Sometimes, while reading these letters, Julia's eyes would fill with tears; delightful tears of love and respect for a sensible and kind-hearted young man. 'Oh, when will he come back to us?' Mrs L. would often say. 'How happy I will be to see him. I will hold him to my heart, along with you, too, Julia!'

Thus months and years passed by. The time came when young master L. was due to return to his homeland and to his mother's embrace. Every day they waited for him and talked about him all the time. As they walked through the flowering meadows (it was already early summer), they kept glancing at the main road. Whenever a cloud of dust rose up in the distance, their hearts, tormented by anticipation, were set a-flutter. They would walk further than usual, linger over lunch, and eat dinner slowly, hoping for the speedy arrival of the much-awaited son and brother (since childhood, Julia had called Eugene her brother).

At long last, he arrived. Exclamations, elation, tears of joy: who could possibly describe such a scene? For several days they were beside themselves with rapture. With the modesty of a well-mannered young lady, Julia tried to restrain the powerful stirrings of her heart, but she did not always succeed. The ardent young man who had grown up with her and loved her as his own sister was eager for her to reaffirm her love after such a long separation. Julia was obliged to behave as freely and simply with him as she had as a child. He was adamant that she must not address him formally, as he could not bear to hear such a thing from the lips of his Julia. 'How unhappy I would be,' he said in an emotional voice, 'if our separation had cooled your love for me, that gentle fire of friendship which was the happiness of my childhood! No, my sister! You love me just as much as you did before; of that my heart is certain. When I parted from you, I ventured into a completely new world, where I was kept occupied and amazed by everything, yet the thought of you both – of my mother and you – was always the foremost and pleasantest thought in my mind. Do you remember how, when we bade each other farewell, your Eugene streamed with tears as he told you in a faltering voice, 'Julia! I will always be your dearest friend!'? I have never forgotten that moment.'

Julia replied only with a smile, but that smile told him everything. Mrs L. embraced her son and Julia joyfully.

The ladies of the house took Eugene to all the best places around the village and showed him the beautiful views from the green hilltops. 'You used to sit with Julia beneath this tall elm tree,' Mrs L. told him. 'You and she would often run through that archway. We would gather wild strawberries in those woods, and when Julia was sad because she couldn't find any berries, you would sneak up behind her and tip your berries into her basket. In that valley over there, you once made me cry and give thanks to God. Do you remember? No, you have forgotten all about it. In that case, I will tell you everything. We once went walking in the grove. When we came out into the valley, we saw an old man lying on the grass, barely able to breathe from exhaustion and the heat. You ran over to him at once, then took off your hat and collected some water in it. You returned to the man, gave him some of the water to drink, and washed the dust off his face, while Julia dried him with her scarf. My goodness! How I rejoiced to see such signs of sensitivity in your heart!'

Walking in the moonlight, they gazed at the starry sky and marvelled at the greatness of God. As they listened to the sound of a waterfall, they talked about immortality. Animated by the spirit of nature, they shared so many lofty, innocent thoughts with each other! The young man's heart was so enraptured upon beholding the image of peaceful innocence in Julia's face as it was illuminated by the silent moonbeams.

Eugene gave Julia lots of sheet music as a gift, together with many French, Italian and German books. She sang and played the harpsichord very well. Klopstock's song *Willkommen, silberner Mond*[2], set to music by the eminent composer Gluck, was particularly to her liking. She could never sing the last verse, in which Gluck had so exquisitely aligned the music with the emotions of the great poet, without feeling something pulling at the strings of her heart. Oh, meek, gentle souls! You alone know the value of these virtuosi, and their immortal compositions are dedicated to you alone. For them, a single one of your tears is the greatest reward.

---

[2] *Welcome, Silver Moon* (German).

On the fifteenth of August, Eugene turned twenty-two, and Julia twenty-one. The dawn chorus woke the young man. He opened his eyes, and everything around him smiled. He rose joyfully and hurried to his mother. She was sitting, lost in thought, leaning on her elbow by the window, outside which a pair of turtle doves were billing and cooing in a young apple tree. Her face bore signs of sublime emotions. Eugene gazed at her with profound respect, not daring to interrupt her musings. Nevertheless, her heart soon sensed the arrival of her beloved son, so she stood up, embraced him, and blessed the day of his birth.

Then Julia arrived. Her light, white dress with pink ribbons, her hair which was let down, and her joyful smile all served to heighten her beauty. She flew into the arms of her guardian. Eugene kissed her hand.

Mrs L. sat down on the sofa and seated her two children beside her. She looked at them with tenderness and love, and began to speak. 'God sees that I love you equally, since my heart recognises Julia as my own daughter. I have always rejoiced at the love you have for each other, and am glad that God has given me such dear children. I admit I was afraid, my son, that, whilst enlightening your mind, your heart, which is so gentle, might be corrupted. Often, on my knees, I have cried out to God, 'Save my son!' He heard my prayer, and you have come back to us with knowledge a-plenty and unspoiled feelings. You have discovered Julia's new accomplishments, have you not? She has been the object of all my care, and I have tried to teach her everything I know. My intention was revealed to God, and now I am revealing it to you. I have been preparing you for each other. You deserve each other; you love each other: complete my happiness and be joined together in an eternal, sacred union!'

Eugene stood up at once, and threw himself at his mother's feet. All he could say was, 'Dearest Mother! Mother!' Julia rested her head on her guardian's chest and squeezed her hand, saying nothing. Eugene put one arm around his mother, and the other around Julia... Oh, those blessed patriarchal times, when a virtuous young man, without any of that apprehensive shyness which indicates a soul corrupted by vice, could embrace a virtuous maiden! One moment flew out of your depths, burst forth from the embrace of eternity which had swallowed you up, and came back into the world, bringing happiness to young Eugene!

'Rejoice, my children!' said Mrs L. 'Rejoice, and make your mother happy!'

'Oh, but am I worthy of such bliss?' said Julia. 'And your kindness...'

'To me, Julia, you are a gift from heaven. A gift which I scarcely dared to wish for, even in the depths of my heart.'

If Raphael had beheld this scene, he would have forgotten his painting and dropped his brush in rapture.

When the servants learned that Eugene was soon to become Julia's husband, they were all overjoyed, since they loved them both. Every one of them hurried to morning prayers, eager to pray with all their hearts for the couple's prosperity. What a spectacle it was for the angels! Eugene and Julia were as one heart, soaring up to heaven on a flame of prayer. Overcome with reverence, Mrs L. fell to her knees many times, raising her eyes heavenwards and then turning to look at her children. It was to be hoped that these heartfelt petitions would have happy consequences for the young couple, and that they would have many years of such uninterrupted bliss as any mortal could possibly enjoy on this earth. However, the destiny that the Almighty has in store for us is an unfathomable mystery. Faithful since time immemorial to the laws of his wisdom and goodness, he creates. Thus we are amazed and awe-inspired, and we must revere him in faith and in silence.

Whilst still in a state of perpetual delight and sublime happiness, Eugene came down with a strong fever towards evening. He tried to ignore it, wanting to overcome nature and hide his struggle, but his condition soon became clear to the observant eyes of his dear mother and Julia. All the nerves in their bodies were filled with fear. Their joy, like the summer sun, was hidden behind a cloud of sad foreboding; storms and thunder lurked in its depths. They put the patient in bed and sent to the town for the doctor. Everyone was anxious, but they still attempted to encourage each other with hope. Some natural impulse – perhaps a fortunate one – makes people act in this way, closing their eyes when the light of future grief begins to shine!

Although the fire of illness was bent on smothering all the life inside Eugene, he nevertheless bade his mother and the tearful Julia be calm, assuring them that he would recover, although the burning in his hands and face belied his words. For three days, during which Mrs L. and Julia barely left his bedside nor even dared take their eyes off him, his sickness ebbed and flowed. The doctor came and examined the patient, but could say nothing definitive. On the fifth day, Eugene seemed much better, and there was a glimmer of relief in those grieving hearts. On the sixth day, though, he lost consciousness, and the doctor confided in Julia that he could not guarantee the young man would survive, citing 'dizziness and fainting!'

In his delirious state, the patient kept saying fervently: 'I cannot leave her! No, I must not! I want to reign with her alone... Leave me, tempter, and do not touch Julia!'

On the ninth day, as dawn was breaking, Eugene's soul left his mortal body. His fraught mother saw a vision wherein the communion of saints took that soul into their embrace, and singing songs at the top of their voices, carried it off into the ether. After this celestial dream, she felt encouraged and able to comfort Julia who had flung herself upon the breast of the deceased and was exclaiming in despair: 'My beloved, my partner! Wait, wait! Let us die together!' She had to be forcibly dragged from the room.

The burial of the body was set to take place three days later. All the domestic staff and peasants alike attended the sad ceremony and wept bitter tears. They all wanted to carry the coffin, thereby paying their last respects to the deceased. The poor mother, wearing a long black dress, walked behind the coffin. Her face was a picture of unspoken grief, yet through the deep traces of this sorrow shone resolution and a firm hope of heavenly succour. Pale, exhausted Julia could not walk unaided, so two women supported her by the arms a short distance from the coffin. Not a single teardrop could be seen in her eyes, and her lips uttered no complaint, but in her heart she felt the full burden of what had occurred.

The mournful tone of the funeral hymns and the sight of the coffin as it was lowered into the ground could not shake the conviction of Mrs L.. Julia, though, unable to bear this final scene, cried out in a loud voice and would have fallen unconscious into the grave, if Mrs L. had not managed to catch hold of her and restrain her.

Thus our admirable young man left this world. Farewell, flower of virtue and innocence! Your remains are at rest in the embrace of the mother of us all, but your spirit, your true being, is sailing through the infinite joys of eternity, waiting for your beloved, with whom it could not be joined in eternal union here on earth. Farewell!

Mrs L. and Julia, deprived of all the happiness of this life, now live in perpetual melancholic solitude. Nature itself, once a source of joy for them, now seems miserable and desolate. Their only solace is found in prayer and thinking about the next life. The following spring, Julia planted many fragrant flowers on the grave of her beloved; watered as they are by her tears, they grow faster than those in the garden or the meadows. The young girls and boys of the village celebrate the coming of fair May near this grave, but their fathers and mothers never pass by without heaving a heavy sigh.

A certain sensitive young man, who was passing through Mrs L.'s village, heard this sad story and visited Eugene's resting place. On a white stone which lay among the flowers on the grave, he wrote with a pencil the following epitaph which was later carved onto a marble slab:

This earth was no place for such a beautiful flower,
So it was borne aloft to a heavenly bower.

Eugénie and Léonce
or *The Ball-gown*
by Madame de Genlis

Mme de Palmène, still young, yet widowed for several years, devoted herself completely to the education of her only daughter who was the object of all her affection as well as all her ministrations. When her husband died, he had left her a large number of debts, and Mme de Palmène had only been able to settle these by reluctantly leaving Paris and moving to an estate which she possessed in Touraine, not far from Loches. The château was ancient and huge. Its drawbridge, moat and towers recalled the memorable era of the likes of du Guesclin and des Bayard, those wonderful days of chivalry which we would no doubt miss if the loyalty and valour of a few proud knights could take the place of the police and the law. The château's interior was in keeping with its exterior. Everything recalled the noble simplicity of our ancestors. There was neither any gilding nor that ridiculous profusion of porcelain objects, figurines and small vases with which our modern houses are filled: instead, there were beautiful tapestries to be admired, depicting interesting aspects of history. There were large galleries to stroll through, hung with family portraits, and from the windows of the sitting room there was a view of a wonderful forest on one side, and the pleasant banks of the river Indre on the other. It was there that Eugénie (that was the name of Mme de Palmène's daughter) spent the first years of her youth, acquiring a taste for country pastimes and a peaceful and secluded lifestyle.

On fine days in spring and summer, she would go for long walks with her mother, and towards evening they would seek out the shade and the coolness of the forest. Sometimes Eugénie would go there to take exercise, and sometimes she would pick the herbs whose names and properties her mother had taught her. She would often take her lessons there, listening to interesting readings; then, as the day was drawing to a close, she would leave the forest and head for the banks of the laughing river. When Eugénie was in her eighth year, she became more sedentary. A thousand activities kept her at the château, but she still rose at dawn, took lunch in the park or the fields, and in the evening she would walk one or two leagues with her mother.

The daughter of her governess was her playmate. This young person, called Valentine, who was four years older than Eugénie, had a cheerful nature; she had a good heart and applied herself well. She was present for all of Eugénie's lessons, and she enjoyed them so much that her young mistress rightly considered her a friend.

Nevertheless, Eugénie reached her sixteenth year. She possessed the gaiety and the innocent graces of her age, a cultivated mind, discretion, unfailing gentleness, and the most perfectly balanced temper. Her affection and appreciation for Mme de Palmène knew no bounds. Always considerate of her mother, and taking every opportunity to please her, there was no task to which she was not drawn. When learning verses by heart, she would tell herself, 'Maman will enjoy listening to me reciting them. I will perform them to her on our walk this evening. She will praise my memory and my hard work.' When she studied English or Italian, she thought, 'It will be such a surprise and a delight for Maman when she sees that I have translated two pages instead of just the one I was given!' When writing, drawing or making music, she had similar thoughts: 'This picture will look nice in Maman's study. Whenever she looks at it, she will think of her Eugénie. This sonata, which I can only play badly at the moment, will charm Maman when I have learned to play it well.' This notion, which she applied to everything, allowed her to find indescribable delight in her studies, smoothing out obstacles and transforming all her tasks into delicious pleasures.

To round off Eugénie's education perfectly, Mme de Palmène decided to spend two years in Paris. At the end of September, she tore herself away from her comfortable solitude and, upon arriving in Paris, she rented a small house where Eugénie often longed for the delightful banks of the Indre and the Loire. Mme de Palmène enjoyed meeting many people whom she had known before. In particular, she sought out an old friend of her husband, the Count of Amilly, whose merits and virtues made him particularly worthy of this preferential treatment. Having been a widower for many years, he only had one son, who was eighteen years old, and from whom he had just parted for two years. This young man, whose name was Léonce, was in Italy, and was later due to travel around the north.

The Count of Amilly came to supper at Mme de Palmène's home every evening, and Eugénie would go to bed at half past ten. As soon as she left, the count would talk about her, always singing her praises. He admired her talents, her modesty, her reserve, and that particular air of gentleness and openness in her nature which infused even her slightest actions with an indescribable charm. Then he would speak of his son, commending his spirit, his character and his heart. Mme de Palmène could not help secretly feeling pleased when she listened to him praising Eugénie, and she could not hear the frequent mentions of Léonce's name without emotion. Thus, during the course of these conversations, the time was forgotten more than once, and she exclaimed more than once in surprise, 'How is that possible? Is it three o'clock already?'

The Count of Amilly continued his frequent visits, but without further explanation. One day, though, he said, 'My son is set to receive a considerable fortune, but before I share it with him, I want to teach him how to enjoy it. When he returns, he will be twenty years old, and I will marry him to a nice woman whose grace, example and gentleness will make all his duties pleasant, and who will give him cause to cherish virtue.'

Mme de Palmène could easily see Eugénie in the description of this woman, but when she reflected upon the extreme discrepancy between her own fortune and that of the Count of Amilly, she could scarcely believe that it was a real prospect for her daughter.

Mme de Palmène had been in Paris for almost two years, and Eugénie was approaching her eighteenth year when, one evening, the Count of Amilly came to visit Mme de Palmène and begged her leave to introduce his son who had just returned. A young man with the most interesting face approached Mme de Palmène and greeted her in a manner which was both eager and timid, and which added to his natural charms. The count and his son stayed for supper. Léonce spoke little, but he looked at Eugénie a lot: every word he did utter showed his keen desire to please Mme de Palmène.

The next day, the count came again with his son, but Mme de Palmène declared that she had made it a firm rule never to receive young people of Léonce's age in her home.

'But Madame,' the count said, 'you must judge for yourself whether that is in your interests…'

'What do you mean?'

'Well, do you not see that his happiness and mine depend on it? Give yourself time to make his acquaintance. If he is fortunate enough to please you, then all my wishes and his will be granted.'

The matter was clear. Mme de Palmène expressed her gratitude to the count for his inspiring speech. Nevertheless, she did not commit to anything, as she wanted to consult Eugénie first, as well as seeking some information about Léonce's character. Everything that she learned only increased her desire to adopt him as her son, so that when the count urged her again to give him an answer, she no longer hesitated. With everyone in agreement, the marriage contract was signed. The next day, it was with great elation that Léonce took the hand of the lovely Eugénie, and the newly wedded couple were taken straight away to a charming estate which belonged to the count, ten leagues from Paris. It was decided that they would not return to Paris until the end of the autumn.

Mme de Palmène spent three months with them. At the end of this time, she was obliged to leave them. Since she was planning to move permanently to Paris, she needed to travel to Touraine to put her affairs in order. Although she would be returning before the winter, it took all of Eugénie's convictions to endure such a painful separation. Her grief and melancholy following her mother's departure only made her more interesting in Léonce's eyes. He found a secret sweetness in contemplating her in such a state of despondency and sadness. Seeing tears pouring down her face, he said to himself, 'What must I owe to possess such a sensitive and appreciative heart?'

Eugénie, however, for fear of upsetting Léonce, hid some of her heartache from him, but she was not so restrained with Valentine, the young girl who had been her companion since childhood. Eugénie found the sweetest consolation in talking about her mother and writing long letters to her every day.

Almost two months had passed since Mme de Palmène's departure, and during that time Eugénie had not travelled to Paris once. Léonce was becoming dearer to her with every passing day. They often went for walks alone together in the woods and fields. Eugénie asked Léonce questions about his travels and tasted the delights of learning as she listened to him. On other occasions, as they sat side by side on the banks of a stream, Eugénie would sing, and her sweet, melodious voice would attract the attention of the harvesters who would leave their work and run over to listen to her. One evening, Eugénie noticed a respectable elderly man among their number. She learned that his name was Jérôme, and although seventy-five years old, he was the sole support for his paralysed sister and five orphaned grandchildren. Eugénie only had a very meagre allowance. Her father-in-law, being a prosperous nobleman, did indeed possess a considerable fortune, but in his wisdom and courage, wishing to give his son and daughter a sense of order and economy, he had not yet shared his wealth with them. 'When you have proved to me,' he had told them, 'that you know how to use money worthily, we will arrange for funds to be shared. In five years, for example, if I am still satisfied with your conduct, I will be pleased to give away my fortune to a son who is economical and sensible; for a fool and a squanderer, however, I will not part with a fortune which belongs to me alone and which I may dispose of as I see fit.'

'Ah, Father!' replied Léonce. 'By giving me Eugénie, have you not already given me everything?'

Eugénie, meanwhile, found her allowance sufficient. She exercised the greatest economy in all things, and still found the means to be generous and charitable. Still preoccupied with the kind old man called Jérôme, when she was going to bed she told Valentine that she would pray that he might be given help.

The next morning, the Count of Amilly came to have lunch with his daughter-in-law, as usual. 'Here is an invitation,' he told her, 'to a magnificent party in Paris in two weeks' time. I would like you to attend. You will need a ball-gown, so I would be pleased to give you one as a gift.'

As he said these words, the count put a purse containing sixty louis on the table. When Eugénie was alone, she called Valentine and showed her the gift that she had just received. 'For fifty louis, I could have a reasonably good dress,' she said. 'So, I am going to take ten louis from this amount and give them to poor Jérôme. You, Valentine, must go into the village and find out whether everything the old man told me is true. If he was not exaggerating when he told me his story, I will take the money to him myself.'

That afternoon, Valentine went back to the village and reported to her young mistress that, not only had she sought information from the priest and some of the villagers, but she had also been inside the old man's hut. There, she had seen the poor paralysed sister who was being looked after by the oldest of Jérôme's grandchildren, a young girl of twelve. The sick woman's room was very clean, and had quite a good bed, while the old man slept on straw in a kind of small barn. Jérôme, it turned out, was the most honest peasant in the village, and the most unfortunate, as well as the best brother and the best grandfather.

'Let us go,' said Eugénie. 'I have with me the purse which my father-in-law gave me. We must take him the ten louis at once.'

Eugénie took Valentine's arm and went out with her, leaving a message for Léonce, who was finishing a game of whist, to let him know that she was going to the willow grove to watch the harvesters working.

When Eugénie arrived at the field where Jérôme usually worked until nightfall, she looked around for him. Not seeing him, she asked where he was. She was told that he had been overcome with heat and exhaustion, so he had gone to rest for a while in the shade and had fallen asleep on the banks of the stream, near a tall briar hedge.

Eugénie and Valentine turned and walked in that direction. They soon saw the old man fast asleep and surrounded by his grandchildren. They approached with caution, for fear of waking him, and came to a halt a few paces away, from where they beheld the most touching scene. The good old man was sleeping soundly. A pretty little girl of eight or nine was carefully tying her apron to the hedge of wild roses above her grandfather's head, in order to shelter him from the sun's heat. One of her brothers was helping her with this, while the other two, armed with willow twigs and kneeling on either side of the old man, were wafting away the craneflies and other flies from around his face. When the little girl spied Eugénie, she gestured to her to be quiet. Eugénie smiled, and approaching on tiptoes, she kissed the girl and said softly to her, 'I need to talk with your grandfather when he wakes up. Go and play with your brothers over there; you can come back when I call you.'

The young girl was reluctant to leave, as were the boys who would only go on condition that Eugénie and Valentine promised to take over the duty of wafting away the flies.

Having agreed to this, Eugénie took the willow twigs and sat with Valentine near the briar hedge, at which point the little family went away and disappeared from view. Then, pulling the purse out of her pocket, Eugénie put it on her lap, ready to count out the ten louis. Worried about making too much noise as she counted the money, she stopped, and casting a glance at the old man, she watched him tenderly. 'He is sleeping so peacefully!' she said. 'He is a good and respectable old man! His face is noble! Seventy is such a venerable age! He has endured so much toil in his long working life, and now that his strength has abandoned him, he is still obliged to labour without respite!'

With these words, Eugénie shed a few tears. 'Madame, just think of the joy,' said Valentine, 'that you will bring him by giving him the ten louis...'

'This gift,' Eugénie added, 'this small sum cannot ensure a happy life for him! Oh, it would be sweet to ensure that he could have peace in his old age! Ten louis would only be a small comfort in his misery, but fifty could put him at ease. Fifty louis! The same as my dress would cost! And what pleasure would I derive from that? It would be scarcely noticed: I would see a thousand more splendid than mine! Besides, Valentine, do you think that Léonce would find me prettier? He praised my face so much today! Yet I only have on a white dress and some cornflowers that he picked this morning. Valentine, with ten louis, I could have a new dress. A simple one, it is true, but it would suit me better: flowers and tulle are more fitting for my age, do you not think?'

'I must admit, Madame, that I would be delighted to see you finely attired.'

'Ah, Valentine, look at this old man, and you will forget such a vain notion. Think of the satisfaction that I will feel by relieving this good father of a family from his poverty! He will dine with such joy this evening, surrounded by his grandchildren! How he will embrace them and receive their caresses! As for me, I will be able to tell my mother about it all tomorrow morning! My mother! How happy she will be when she reads my letter!'

'But Madame, you will be the only person dressed so simply at the party. That would displease your father-in-law...'

'And perhaps Léonce, too... Nevertheless, they are both so good and so kind! Come, Valentine, I will talk with Léonce... I should not do anything without seeking his advice. We must go away from here, because the sight of this old man is a temptation I will not be able to resist. Let us find Léonce: we will come back afterwards.'

As she was saying this, Eugénie was about to stand up when she heard a sound of leaves rustling behind her, making her turn her head. At the same moment she spied Léonce who burst through the hedgerow and threw himself at her feet. A moment after Eugénie's departure, he had left the château to join her. Knowing that she was looking for Jérôme, and not doubting that she was planning to help him, Léonce had come and hidden behind the briar hedgerow, so that he could listen to their conversation, and although Eugénie was only speaking in hushed tones, he had not missed a single word, being but a few paces away. 'My charming Eugénie!' he exclaimed, falling to his knees. 'I heard everything. By concerning yourself with ways to assure this old man's happiness, you have caused mine to overflow. You have taught me how much you deserve to be loved.'

Léonce was still speaking when Jérôme awoke. At once, Eugénie pulled herself away from Léonce's arms and approached the old man. He looked at her in astonishment, and attempted to stand, out of respect for her. Eugénie invited him to remain seated. He excused himself, adding, 'I must go to work.'

'No,' said Eugénie. 'Have a rest today...'

'What about my day's wage?'

'I will pay you. Here, take this purse: may receiving it bring you as much pleasure as giving it brings to me!'

With these words, she leaned over affectionately and respectfully, and placed the purse containing the fifty louis into the old man's trembling hands. Léonce watched Eugénie in rapture: never had she seemed so charming to him; never had she made such a profound impression on his heart.

However, when the old man opened the purse, he found himself in a state of shock. He had never seen such a huge sum in all his life. He rubbed his eyes and thought he was dreaming. Eugénie silently rejoiced at the untold success of her surprise. Eventually, Jérôme put his hands firmly together and said in a faltering voice, 'But, dear God, what have I done to deserve such a generous gift?'

Lifting his head, he looked at Eugénie, his eyes filled with tears. 'Oh, Madame,' he exclaimed, 'may the Lord reward you by blessing you with children like yourself!'

Silenced by his tears, he could say no more. At that moment, Jérôme's grandchildren all came running back. Eugénie begged the old man to close the purse and say nothing to anyone about what had happened. She kissed pretty little Simonette one more time, and bidding farewell to the good old man, she set off with Léonce along the road to the château.

Because of her natural sensitivity, Eugénie did not want her father-in-law to find out about what she had done until the day of the party, for fear that the count might give her another ball-gown. The day finally arrived. The count stayed in the country, while Léonce and Eugénie set off for Paris. At the ball, Eugénie attracted and held everyone's gaze, not only as a result of her personal charms, but also through the elegant simplicity of her attire, which was enhanced with neither diamonds nor pearls: nothing eclipsed her natural grace. The sweet memory of the old man kept returning to her mind, bringing fresh happiness, and on more than one occasion she contemplated the excessive and foolish opulence of her young peers and thought to herself, 'How I feel sorry for them! They do not know real pleasure!'

At daybreak, Léonce took Eugénie back to the country. He wanted his father to see her dressed for the ball, being eager to tell him the story of the old man, and he anticipated with delight the pleasure which his father would derive from this. The count did indeed listen to the story with a mixture of affection and joy. He hugged the lovely Eugénie a thousand times and from that moment onwards, he felt the most tender paternal feelings towards her.

The next day, Eugénie and Léonce went to visit the old man. Léonce told him that he would secure the futures of two of the children; the pretty little Simonette and her second brother. Simonette was sent to a seamstress in Paris, and her brother was given an apprenticeship with a carpenter. The old man's joy knew no bounds when the count of Amilly gave him a cow and an acre of land next to his cottage. Eugénie's delighted mother, Mme de Palmène, received the letter containing all the details as she was travelling back from Touraine.

My children, at your age it is impossible to imagine the effect that such a letter can have on a mother's heart! At last, the tender-hearted and charming Eugénie found herself in the arms of Mme de Palmène, who never left her daughter again. Eugénie always brought joy to her mother, her husband and her family; in her heart and in the appreciation of others, she found the just reward for her virtues and her actions, and her happiness was made complete when heaven granted the old man's wishes: she had the children she deserved, and they allowed her to taste that same happiness which she had given to her own mother.

The Nightingale
by Nikolai Mikhailovich Karamzin

What is the sound that rings abroad
from the treetops in the moon's clear light?
What sweetness into heart and soul is poured
amidst the stillness of the night,
when Nature falls silent for a time
and the stars in the blue vault of heaven
in the mirror of a stream do shine?
What is it that cheers the sadness in my bosom,
and meekly my spirit regales?
The gentle voice of the sweet nightingale!

Dear singer, friend of Orpheus!
Who can give you fitting praise?
The green forests' Coryphaeus,
in a song of self-glory your voice you raise.
Your hymns of praise to Nature abound,
in honour of your dearest Mother.
Your match or equal as yet unfound,
you defy envy any sound to utter!

Ah! The woods are filled with songs so tender;
but what are they compared to your own?
Like golden Phoebus, appearing in splendour
in the firmament, and whose glory alone
causes the moon and stars to seem dimmer,
your song renders insignificant
the harmony of all other singers.

The lark's song, too, is brilliant,
twisting beneath dark clouds bearing rain.
Even in captivity the robin's song is delightful;
of love in the springtime is his refrain[3],
while the linnet and siskin ever cheerful,
the tiny warbler and the bunting,
and the goldfinch in its beauty most rare,
all of them sweetly and harmoniously sing,
and all are pleasing to the ear;
but although each song is lovely and appealing,
compared to yours it is as nothing!
They capture only one emotion at a time,
while your rapturous heart everything combines.
They are muses, but you are divine!

What a wonderful art you embody!
At first, like a pipe playing in the distance,
gently, you begin to sing softly,
making everything stop to listen;
starting with a pleasant whistle and a warbling –
then, raising your voice ever higher,
and bringing feeling to life with feeling,
you direct your song like a river:
wave after wave, on it goes,
easily, freely, unconstrained,
so brisk are your arpeggios,
each merging into the next, in a chain;
you peal... and then you fade away;
like a languid stream you babble;
as gentle as a breeze in the month of May,

---

[3] The Comte de Bouffon called the robin the 'bird of love'.

your sigh is tender, kind and gentle...
From your heart every sound bursts in grandeur,
and to another heart softly surrenders...

Such a passionate, happy husband is he
(faithful friend, ardent lover),
telling his dear wife tunefully
of his burning love, his heart's fire.
The power of your voice is astonishing —
a wonderful gift from Mother Nature —
gently the soul's defences penetrating
tenderly nourishing with its favours,
thus making it a hundred times greater.

Sing, my friend! Enraptured by you,
at the quiet hour, under cover of night,
an unhappy person, shedding a sweet tear or two,
makes peace with heaven and with fate;
the captive's chains are forgotten,
in his heart having found freedom,
he realises he can bear his burden.

One who weeps at a graveside
(where dust, by soul and heart much treasured
in silent stillness there abides,
in a slumber deep and blessed),
upon hearing you finds comfort and solace
with eternal life's hopeful promise,
and everlasting love, dear and precious.

In that place where happiness lies;
where the senses feel only joy;

where the heart knows no sighs;
where my tender Agathon, innocent boy,
like a May hyacinth so charming,
blooms in immortality's spring...
There a smile for me is waiting!

Sing, my friend! Enraptured by you,
and by Nature and the lovely spring healed,
I will thus forget my woe.
The scents of flowers in the fields
will soothe my breast and end its sorrow.
When the son of Phoebus, winged peace, descends,
from the heavens above to the earth below,[4]
thunder and peoples will fall silent in the end.
Tears will be dried by the olive tree,
then, Nature's Orpheus, will I pour
my heart into an anthem sweet
and join my song of peace with yours!

---

[4] Written in time of war.

Part 2: Liza

Poor Liza is probably the most popular of Karamzin's sentimental tales. Published in 1792, three years later than *Eugene and Julia*, it has an extra layer of complexity, with some of the sweetness soured, and some of the light darkened. It tells of two contrasting characters; Liza who, like Eugene and Julia, is the embodiment of purity, and Erast, a fairy-tale-style villain whose sole aim is to seduce Liza, only to abandon her straight afterwards. The first part of the story is idyllic, when the young couple meet and fall in love, but as soon as Liza's innocence is taken away, things begin to fall apart. As with other Sentimentalist writing, the setting reflects what is happening in the story, but there are also plenty of contrasts here, too, for example between town and country, wealth and poverty, good weather and bad, and most importantly between peasantry and nobility. Once again, flowers and nature play an important role, foreshadowing and echoing events, and water features in many scenes; flowing, mirroring, bringing and carrying away.

This time, the narrator is more apparent than in *Eugene and Julia*, and effectively a character in his own right. He is present at the beginning and the end of the story, visiting the scene where the action took place, and also adds his own commentary on events from time to time.

Poor Liza is followed here by two poems and a story. The first of the two poems, *The Nosegay*, was written by the German Sentimentalist poet, Salomon Gessner, whose work Karamzin both read and translated. The nosegay in this story is reminiscent of the flowers picked by Liza, but although the two stories have much in common, Ida's does not end quite so tragically as Liza's.

I wrote the second poem, *Eternal Memory,* after reading about 'Liza's pond' at the site of the former Simonov Monastery, and how it became a place of literary pilgrimage for a while, following the popularity of the story. I was also intrigued by the idea of the narrator's meeting with Erast and visiting Liza's grave, and wondered what that place might be like, and whether the two were reconciled in the afterlife...

Since Alexander Pushkin's *The Stationmaster* was written in response to the Sentimentalist style, and contains references to *Poor Liza* in varying degrees of obliqueness, it made sense to include it in this collection. Pushkin being possibly Russia's best-loved writer, this story has, of course, been widely translated, and I deliberated for a long time over whether to include one of the numerous excellent English versions already in existence, or whether to have a go at translating it myself. To attempt to redo what so many eminent translators have already done very well seemed like madness, but for better or worse, I decided to do it anyway, as I know no deeper way of exploring a text than to translate it. Hopefully, despite its possible shortcomings, my version will be in keeping with the other translations in this collection, making comparisons easier.

Pushkin's all-too short life (1799-1837) overlapped that of Karamzin (1766-1826) by several years, and his writing uses Karamzin's achievements as a springboard, taking Russian literature from where his pioneering predecessor left off and developing it further. *Eugene Onegin*, a novel in verse, and perhaps Pushkin's greatest work, contains echoes of *Poor Liza*, as it tells of a girl who is pursued by a young man of questionable morals. Even more parallels, though, can be drawn with *The Stationmaster*: this story is clearly more sophisticated and complex than its Karamzinian prototype, but Minsky the hussar is of a similar mindset to Erast, the narrator is a definite presence and freely interjects with his own opinions, and Dunya, like Liza, is led astray, although she does appear to be rather more worldly and perhaps not quite so innocent.

Poor Liza
by Nikolai Mikhailovich Karamzin

It is possible that no-one living in Moscow knows the city as well as I do, since no-one is out and about as much as I, no-one wanders around on foot more than I do, without a plan, aimlessly – wherever the fancy takes me – through meadows and groves, over hills and plains. Every summer I find new and delightful places, or new beauty in old ones.

The place which I find most pleasant of all, however, is where the sombre, gothic towers of the Si..nov Monastery stand tall. From atop that hill, you can see almost all of Moscow to your right, a terrible mass of houses and churches which presents itself to the eyes in the form of a majestic *amphitheatre*: a marvellous scene, especially when the sun shines upon it, the evening light glowing on the countless golden cupolas and crosses ascending to the heavens! Down below stretch rich, lush green meadows of flowers, and beyond them, bordered by yellow sands, flows a gleaming river, stirred up by the gentle oars of fishing boats, or churned beneath the rudders of the laden river vessels which sail from the fertile lands of the Russian Empire to supply greedy Moscow with grain. On the other side of the river there is a grove of oak trees, near which a large flock of sheep grazes: sitting in the shade of the trees, young shepherds sing mournful songs and while away the summer days which, for them, are all the same. A little further away, among the dense greenery of ancient elms, glimmers the golden-domed Danilov Monastery, and beyond that, almost on the edge of the horizon, is the bluish hue of Sparrow Hills. To the left lie vast fields of wheat, woodlands, three or four villages, and in the distance, the Kolomenskoye estate with its lofty palace.

I am a frequent visitor to this place, and I almost always welcome in the spring here. I also come in the sombre days of autumn to grieve with nature. The winds howl terribly within the walls of the deserted monastery, among the overgrown graves, and in the dark passages alongside the cells. There, as I lean on the ruins of the gravestones, I listen to the muffled groan of a time that has been swallowed by the abyss of the past – a groan which makes my heart shudder and tremble. Sometimes I go inside the cells and imagine those who once lived there -- such mournful scenes! Here, I see a grey-haired elderly monk kneeling before a crucifix and praying for a speedy release from his earthly bonds, as all the pleasure has gone from his life and his feelings have faded away, apart from pain and weakness. Over there, a young brother, pale-faced and with a weary gaze, is looking through the grille on the window at a field, where he sees happy birds swimming freely in the sea of the air. He watches them, and he sheds bitter tears. He languishes, withers and shrivels, then the dismal ringing of the bells informs me of his untimely death. Sometimes, at the gates of the church, I contemplate the mural depicting the miracles which have taken place in this monastery: in one place, fish fall from the sky to feed the inhabitants of the monastery as it is besieged by numerous enemies; in another the image of the Mother of God is causing enemies to flee. This all reminds me of the history of our fatherland; the sad story of those times when fierce Tatars and Lithuanians laid waste to the area around the Russian capital with fire and sword, and when unfortunate Moscow, like a defenceless widow, turned to God alone for help at times of such terrible disaster.

However, what draws me most often to the walls of the Si...nov monastery is my recollection of Liza's sorry fate. Poor Liza! Ah, how I love those subjects which touch my heart and cause me to shed tears of tender sorrow!

Seventy sazhens, or a couple of hundred yards from the monastery walls, near a birch grove, in the middle of a green meadow, stands an empty hut with no door, windows or floor, and whose roof has long since rotted and collapsed. It was in this hut, some thirty or so years ago, that the lovely, good-natured Liza lived with her elderly mother.

Liza's father had been a relatively prosperous peasant, since he loved work, tilled the land well and led a wholly sober life. Soon after his death, though, his wife and daughter become destitute. Their lazy hired hand was a poor labourer in the fields, so the wheat no longer flourished. They were compelled to rent out their land for a mere pittance. What was more, the poor widow, who wept almost constantly over the death of her husband (even peasants know how to love!), became ever frailer with each passing day, and could not work at all. Only Liza, who was fifteen years old when her father departed, worked alone day and night, regardless of her tender youth and rare beauty, weaving canvases, knitting stockings, gathering flowers in the spring and berries in the summer, and selling them in Moscow. The sensitive, kind old woman, seeing how exhausted her daughter was, often clasped the girl to her feebly beating heart and called her divine mercy, a breadwinner, and comfort in her old age, and implored God to reward her for all that she had done for her mother.

'God gave me hands that I might work,' Liza said. 'You fed me from your own breast and looked after me when I was a child, and now my turn has come to look after you. Do not grieve and weep: our tears will not bring my father back.'

Nevertheless, gentle Liza herself frequently struggled to hold back her own tears. She remembered, alas, that she had once had a father, and that he had passed away, but in order to console her mother, she tried to conceal the sorrow in her heart and appear calm and happy.

'I will cry no more, my dear Liza,' the grief-stricken old woman replied, 'when I am in the next world. They say that everyone will be happy there. I will probably find happiness when I see your father. I do not wish to die yet, though: what would become of you without me? With whom could I leave you? No, God willing, you must be comfortably settled first of all! Perhaps we will find a kind man soon. Then, having given my blessing to both of you, my dear children, I will make the sign of the cross and rest in peace in the damp earth.'

Two years had passed since the death of Liza's father. The meadows were filled with flowers, and Liza arrived in Moscow carrying lilies-of-the-valley. In the street, she happened upon a young, well-dressed gentleman of kindly appearance. She showed him the flowers... and blushed.

'Are you selling these, young lady?' he asked with a smile.

'Yes, I am,' she replied.

'How much would you like for them?'

'Five kopeks.'

'That's too cheap. Here's a rouble.'

Surprised, Liza dared to look up at the young man. Then she blushed even more, and looking down at the ground, told him that she couldn't accept a rouble.

'Whyever not?'

'I do not need more.'

'Well, I think that beautiful lilies-of-the-valley, handpicked by a beautiful girl, are worth a rouble. But since you will not take it, here are your five kopeks. I would like to always buy your flowers: pick them only for me.'

Liza gave him the flowers, took the five kopeks, curtsied, and was about to go, but the stranger took her by the arm to stop her.

'Where are you going, young lady?'

'Home.'

'Where is your home?'

Liza told him where she lived, and then left. The young man did not attempt to detain her, perhaps because passers-by were stopping to look and sneer at them.

When Liza arrived home, she told her mother what had happened.

'You were right not to accept the rouble. He might be a bad man...'

'Oh no, Mother! I do not think so. He had such a kind face, and his voice...'

'In any case, Liza, it is best to feed oneself through the fruits of one's own labours and not accept charity. My dear, you have no idea how evil people may harm a poor young woman! My heart lurches every time you go into the city; I always light a candle in front of the icon and pray to the Lord God to preserve you from all trouble and misfortune.'

Liza's eyes filled with tears, and she kissed her mother.

The next day, Liza picked the very best lilies-of-the-valley and took them, once again, into the city. Her eyes silently cast around, searching. Many people wanted to buy her flowers, but she replied that they were not for sale, and looked this way and that. Evening came, when she must return home, and the flowers were tossed into the Moskva River.

'You belong to no-one!' said Liza, feeling such sadness in her heart.

The following evening Liza was seated by the window, spinning and singing plaintive songs in a soft voice, when she suddenly leapt up and exclaimed, 'Oh!'

The young stranger was standing beneath the window.

'What is the matter?' asked Liza's startled mother who was sitting nearby.

'Nothing, Mother,' Liza replied timidly. 'It is just that I saw him.'

'Whom?'

'The gentleman who bought my flowers.'

The old woman looked out of the window. The young man bowed to her so courteously and with such a pleasant air that she could only think good of him.

'Greetings, dear old lady!' he said. 'I am very tired; I don't suppose you have any fresh milk, do you?'

Liza, being obliging, and not waiting for her mother's response – perhaps because she already knew what it would be – ran to the cellar and brought back a clean jug covered with a spotless wooden lid, then she reached for a glass, rinsed it, dried it with a white towel, filled it up, and handed it through the window, her eyes downcast all the while.

The stranger drank, and nectar from the hands of Hebe could not have seemed sweeter to him. As anyone might suppose, he thanked Liza afterwards, and not only with words, but also with his eyes. Meanwhile, the kind-hearted older woman told him all about her grief and consolation; about the death of her husband and her daughter's endearing virtues, such as her conscientiousness, gentleness, and so on. He listened attentively to her, but his eyes were... Well, need I say where?

As for Liza... Timid Liza glanced occasionally at the young man, but swifter than lightning which flashes then disappears behind a cloud, her blue eyes looked back down at the ground as soon as they encountered his gaze.

'I would be much obliged,' he told her mother, 'if your daughter did not sell her handiwork to anyone but me. That way, she would not need to go into the city so frequently, and you would not have to be separated from her. I could come to your house from time to time.'

At that, Liza's eyes shone with joy, which she tried in vain to hide. Her cheeks glowed like the sunset on a clear summer's evening as she looked at her left sleeve, clutching it with her right hand. The old woman eagerly accepted this offer, not suspecting anything untoward, and she assured the stranger that the linen woven by Liza, as well as the stockings she knitted, were especially good and harder-wearing than any others.

It was growing dark, and the young man was preparing to leave.

'What should we call you, dear, kind Sir?' asked the old woman.

'My name is Erast,' he replied.

'Erast,' Liza said softly. 'Erast!' She repeated the name five times, as if trying to commit it to memory.

Erast bade them farewell, then left. Liza followed him with her eyes, while her mother sat, lost in thought until, taking her daughter by the hand, the old woman said, 'Ah Liza! How good and kind he is! If only you could have a husband like that!'

Liza's heart was all aflutter.

'Mother! Mother! How could that be? He is a gentleman, and among peasants...' Liza never finished her sentence.

At this point, the reader should know that this young man, Erast, was a rather rich nobleman, of reasonable intellect and with a good heart which, although kind by nature, was also weak and fickle.

He led an indulgent lifestyle, thinking only of his own pleasure, and seeking it in worldly amusements but frequently not finding it, resulting in his feeling bored and complaining about his lot. Liza's beauty had made an impression on his heart from their first meeting. He read novels and idylls, possessed a somewhat lively imagination, and often transported himself in his thoughts to bygone days (real or otherwise) where, if the poets are to be believed, everyone wandered carefree through meadows, bathed in pure springs, kissed like turtle doves, relaxed beneath rose bushes and myrtles, and spent all of their days in joyous idleness. It seemed to him that he had found in Liza that which his heart had long been seeking. 'Nature is calling me into its embrace, and to its pure joys,' he thought, and resolved – for a while, at least – to abandon high society.

Let us return to Liza. Night was drawing in, so the mother blessed her daughter and wished her sweet dreams, but this time her wish did not come true: Liza did not sleep well at all. A new visitor to her heart, the image of Erast, presented itself so vividly that she woke up almost every minute, opening her eyes and sighing. Liza rose before the sun, walked out to the banks of the Moskva River, sat down on the grass, and filled with melancholy, gazed at the white mists which swirled in the air and then lifted, leaving sparkling drops on nature's green carpet.

Silence reigned all around. Soon, though, the rising luminary of the daytime roused all of creation: the groves and bushes came to life, birds flitted about and began to sing, and flowers raised their heads to drink in the life-giving rays of light. Liza, however, remained seated, still full of sadness.

Oh, Liza! Liza! What has happened to you? You used to wake with the birds, rejoicing with them at the morning, and your pure, joyful soul would shine in your eyes, just as the sun shines in the drops of heavenly dew; but now you are pensive and your heart does not know nature's joy.

Meanwhile, a young shepherd was herding his flock along the riverbank and playing on his pipe. Liza watched him intently and thought: 'Ah, if only the man who is occupying my thoughts had been born a simple peasant or a shepherd, and if only it was he who was driving his flock past me right now! Oh, how I would curtsey to him with a smile and greet him, saying, 'Hello, dear shepherd! Where are you taking your sheep? There is green grass for your sheep here, as well as red flowers that you can use to make a garland for your hat.' He would gaze tenderly at me, and perhaps even take my hand... But that is just a dream!' The shepherd, still playing his pipe, walked on by and disappeared with his motley flock behind a nearby hill.

Suddenly, Liza heard the sound of oars. Glancing at the river, she saw a boat, and in the boat was Erast.

Blood began to rush through every vein in her body, but not out of fear, of course. She stood up and tried to walk but could not. Erast leapt out onto the bank, approached Liza, and her dreams partly came true, as *he gazed tenderly at her and took her by the hand...* Meanwhile, Liza stood there with downcast eyes, her cheeks burning and her heart fluttering, unable to withdraw her hand or turn away when he approached her with his rose-coloured lips... Ah! So ardently did he kiss her that the whole universe seemed to be on fire!

'Dear Liza!' said Erast. 'Dear Liza! I love you.' These words resounded in the depths of her soul, like rapturous, heavenly music, so that she could scarcely believe her ears and...

At this point, I will set aside my paintbrush. I will merely say that, in that moment of rapture, Liza's shyness vanished. Erast knew that he was loved; loved passionately by a new, pure and open heart.

They sat on the grass in such a way that there was little space between them, gazing into each other's eyes and saying, '*Love me!*', and two hours passed in an instant. Eventually, Liza realised that her mother might be worried about her. It was time to part.

'Oh, Erast!' she said. 'Will you always love me?'

'Always, my dear Liza. Always!' he replied.

'Can you swear it?'

'Yes, I can, dear Liza. I can!'

'No! There is no need for oaths. I believe you Erast; I do. Why would you deceive poor Liza? Surely that could never be!'

'Never, never, dear Liza!'

'I am so happy, and my mother will be overjoyed, too, when she finds out that you love me!'

'Oh, no, Liza! There is no need to tell her anything.'

'Why not?'

'Old people can be suspicious. She might imagine something terrible.'

'That would not happen.'

'Still, I beg you not to tell her a word about this.'

'Very well. I will do as you say, although I do not like to keep secrets from her.'

They bade each other farewell, kissed, and promised one last time to meet every evening, whether on the riverbank, in the birch grove, or somewhere near Liza's home, just as long as they always saw each other. Liza went away, but her eyes turned back a hundred times to look at Erast who was still standing on the bank and watching as she departed.

Liza returned to her hut in quite a different state to that in which she had left. On her face and in all her movements there was heartfelt joy.

'He loves me!' she thought with delight.

'Oh, dearest Mama!' Liza said to her mother who had only just woken up. 'Oh, dearest Mama, it is such a wonderful morning! It is so joyful out in the fields! The larks have never sung so well, the sun has never shone so brightly, and the flowers have never smelled so lovely!'

Propping herself up with a walking stick, the old woman went out into the meadow to enjoy the morning that Liza had described so prettily and colourfully. It was indeed, she discovered, particularly pleasant; her sweet daughter had cheered up all of nature with her own happiness. 'Ah, Liza!' she said. 'How good is the work of our Almighty God! For nearly sixty years I have lived on this earth, and I still never tire of looking upon the Lord's creation; at the pure sky like a huge canopy, and at the ground which is covered with new grass and flowers every year. The King of Heaven must surely have loved humanity when he chose this world for us. Oh Liza! Who would ever want to die, were it not for the occasional grief that comes our way? Clearly, it is essential. We might forget our souls if we never shed any tears.'

But Liza thought: 'Ah! I would sooner forget my soul than forget my beloved!'

After that, Erast and Liza, for fear of not keeping their word, met every evening (when Liza's mother had gone to bed), sometimes on the riverbank or among the silver birches, but most often in the shade of the hundred-year old oaks (eighty or so sazhens [5] from the hut). These oak trees overshadowed a deep pond of pure water, which had been dug out in ancient times. There, the quiet moon would often shine its silver beams through the green branches and onto Liza's fair hair where the winds played along with the hand of her sweetheart. These same moonbeams would frequently light up the glimmering tears of love which always appeared in Liza's gentle eyes when Erast kissed her. They embraced, but chaste, shy Cynthia had no need to hide away from them behind a cloud, since their embraces were pure and innocent.

'When you...' Liza said to Erast. 'Ah, when you tell me, *I love you, my dearest!* and when you clasp me to your heart and gaze at me with your adorable eyes,

---

[5] A unit of measurement. One sazhen is approximately 2.13 metres.

then I feel so good that I forget myself. I forget everything... except Erast. It is wonderful! It is a marvel, my love, that I was able to live so peacefully and happily without knowing you! Now I cannot comprehend it, because life without you would not be life, but sadness and tedium. Without your eyes, the bright moon is dark; without your voice, the song of the nightingale is dull; without your breath, the breeze is intolerable.'

Erast delighted in his shepherdess, as he called Liza, and seeing how much she loved him made him feel even more admirable. All the glittering amusements of high society paled into insignificance in comparison with the pleasures with which this *passionate friendship* with an innocent soul filled his heart. It was with disgust that he thought about the despicable wantonness in which he had formerly indulged his senses. 'I will live with Liza, as a brother with a sister,' he thought. 'I will not abuse her love, and I will be forever happy!'

Foolish young man! Do you not know your own heart? Do you always take responsibility for your actions? Does reason always govern your emotions?

Liza demanded that Erast visit her mother often. 'I love her,' she said, 'and I wish her well, and I think that seeing you would bring pleasure to anyone.'

The old woman really was pleased to see him. She loved to talk to him about her late husband and about her younger days; how she met her dear Ivan, how he loved her with such love, and how she had agreed to live with him. 'Ah, we never tired of gazing at each other, until the moment when cruel death knocked him off his feet. He died in my arms!'

Erast listened to her with unfeigned pleasure. He bought Liza's handiwork from her and offered to pay ten times more than the price that was asked, but the old woman would never take more than was owed.

Several weeks passed in this way. One evening, Erast waited a long time for Liza to arrive. Eventually she came, but she was so unhappy that he was afraid; her eyes were red from crying.

'Liza, Liza! What has happened to you?'

'Ah, Erast! I have been crying!'

'Why? What is the matter?'

'I must tell you everything. A young man, the son of a rich peasant from a nearby village, is trying to win my affection. Mother wants me to marry him.'

'Will you say yes?'

'You are so cruel! How can you ask such a thing? I feel sorry for my mother; she keeps crying and saying that I do not care about her peace of mind, and that she will worry herself to death if she cannot marry me off. Ah! My mother does not know what a dear companion you are to me!'

Erast kissed Liza, saying that her happiness was dearer to him than anything on earth, and that when her mother died, he would take Liza with him and live with her inseparably, in a village deep in the middle of the forest, as if in paradise.

'But you cannot be my husband!' Liza said, sighing softly.

'Why not?'

'I am a peasant.'

'You offend me. What matters most to your beloved is a sensitive, innocent soul, and Liza will always be closest to my heart.'

She threw herself into his arms, and at that moment purity was set to perish! Erast sensed an unusual stirring in his blood. Never had Liza seemed so charming as she did now… never had her caresses had such a powerful effect on him… never had her kisses seemed so ardent. She knew nothing, suspected nothing, feared nothing. The darkness of the night fed his desires, since not a single star was shining in the sky, and there was not the slightest glimmer to shed any light on this transgression.

Erast felt a trembling within. Liza felt the same, not knowing why, not knowing what was happening to her... Ah Liza! Liza! Where is your guardian angel? Where is your innocence?

The misdemeanour was over a moment later. Liza could not fathom her emotions, and asked questions in her bewilderment. Erast said nothing – he searched for the right words but did not find them.

'Oh, I am afraid,' said Liza. 'I am afraid of what has happened to us! I felt as if I was dying, and that my soul... No, I do not know how to say it! Why are you so quiet, Erast? Why are you sighing? Oh, my goodness! What is happening?'

Meanwhile, lightning flashed and thunder rumbled. Liza was shaking all over.

'Erast, Erast!' she said. 'I am frightened! I am afraid that the thunder might kill me for my crimes!'

The storm raged menacingly, rain poured from black clouds, and it seemed as if nature was lamenting Liza's lost innocence.

Erast attempted to calm Liza, and took her back home. Tears streamed from her eyes as she bade him farewell. 'Oh, Erast! Tell me that we will be as happy as we were before!'

'We will, Liza. We will!' he replied.

'Please God! I cannot believe what you say, even though I love you! But in my heart... Enough! Forgive me! Tomorrow... tomorrow we will see each other again.'

They continued to meet each other, but everything had changed so much! Erast was no longer content with Liza's innocent caresses alone; with her loving eyes, the touch of her hands, her kisses, and her pure embraces. He wanted more and more, until there was nothing else to want. Anyone who knows his own heart and who has contemplated the delicate nature of his own pleasure, will of course, agree with me, that the fulfilment of *all* desires is the most perilous temptation of love. To Erast, Liza was no longer the immaculate angel who had fired his imagination and delighted his soul. Platonic love had given way to certain feelings in which he could take no *pride*, but which were not new to him. As for Liza, having given herself to him completely, she lived and breathed like a lamb, always obedient to his will and finding her own happiness in his pleasure. She noticed a change in him, and often told him: 'You were happier before. We used to be more at ease and contented, and I was not afraid that I might lose your love!'

Sometimes, as he bade her farewell, he would say, 'Tomorrow, Liza, I cannot meet you. An important matter has arisen,' and Liza would sigh every time he uttered these words.

Eventually, she went five days without seeing him, and she was greatly perturbed. On the sixth day, he arrived with a forlorn expression and told her, 'Dearest Liza, I must say goodbye to you for a while. As you know, we are at war, and the regiment to which I belong is going on a campaign.'

Liza turned pale and almost fainted.

Erast caressed her, declaring that he would always love his darling Liza, and that upon his return, he hoped they would never be parted again. She was silent for a long time, then her eyes streaming with bitter tears, she clutched his hand, glanced at him with all the tenderness of love, and asked, 'Can you really not stay?'

'I could,' he replied, 'but only with the greatest disgrace. My honour would be severely blemished. Everyone would despise me and disdain me as a coward and an unworthy son of the fatherland.'

'Well, in that case,' said Liza, 'you must go. Go wherever God commands! But you could be killed.'

'To die for one's country is not terrible, dearest Liza.'

'If you leave this world, then I shall die at once.'

'Why give that any thought? I hope to remain alive, and return to you, my dearest.'

'Please God! Please God! I will pray for that every hour of every day. Oh, if only I could read and write! Then you could tell me about everything that happens to you, and I could write to you about my tears!'

'No. Look after yourself, Liza. Take care of yourself for the sake of your beloved. I do not want you to cry over me.'

'You are so cruel! Do you mean to deny me that comfort? No! When I am parted from you, I will only stop crying when my heart runs dry.'

'Think of the wonderful moment when we will see each other again.'

'I will. I will think about that! Oh, if only it could come quickly! My dearest, darling Erast! Remember your poor Liza who loves you more than herself!'

Alas, I cannot describe everything that they talked about on this occasion. The next day was to be their last meeting.

Erast wanted to say goodbye to Liza's mother who could not hold back her tears upon hearing that her *kind, comely gentleman* must go off to war. He urged her to take some money from him, saying, 'While I am away, I do not want Liza to sell any of her handiwork which by agreement belongs to me.'

The old woman showered him with blessings. 'Please God,' she said, 'you will return to us safely, and I will see you again in this life! Perhaps by that time Liza will have found herself a suitable husband. How I would thank the Lord if you could join us for the wedding! When Liza has children, you must be godfather to them, Sir! Oh, I really do hope I live to see that day!'

Liza stood beside her mother, not daring to look at her. The reader can easily imagine what she was feeling at that moment.

But what must she have felt when Erast embraced her and clutched her to his breast for the last time, saying, 'Forgive me, Liza!'? What a moving scene! The glow of dawn, like a sea of scarlet, flooded the eastern sky. Erast stood beneath the branches of the tall oak tree, his pale, grief-stricken companion languishing in his arms, bidding farewell not only to him, but also to her heart. All of nature fell silent.

Liza sobbed. Erast wept. He let go of her. She fell onto her knees, raised her arms heavenwards and watched as Erast went away, further and further, until at last he disappeared from view. The sun began to shine, and poor abandoned Liza took leave of her senses and her mind.

When she came round, the world itself seemed desolate and mournful. All the delights of nature had been hidden from her along with the love of her heart. 'Ah,' she thought. 'Why am I left behind in this wilderness? What is preventing me from hastening after my dear Erast? War does not frighten me: my only fear is being wherever my beloved is not. I want to live with him and die with him, or let my death save his precious life. Wait, wait, my darling! I will fly to you!'

She was ready to run after Erast, but one thought prevented her: 'I have a mother!' Liza sighed, and bowing her head, walked back to the hut, treading softly.

From that moment onwards, her days were spent in grief and yearning, which she had to conceal from her dear mother, although this merely made her heart suffer all the more! The only relief came when Liza retreated into the depths of the forest, where she could freely shed her tears and lament her separation from her beloved. The melancholy turtledove often joined its own plaintive voice to her wailing. Sometimes, though – albeit extremely rarely – a golden ray of hope and comfort shone through the darkness of her sorrow. 'When he returns to me, I will be so happy! Everything will change!' These thoughts brightened her eyes and refreshed the rosiness of her cheeks, and Liza would smile like a May morning after a stormy night. About two months passed in this way.

One day, Liza had to go to Moscow to buy some rose water to soothe her mother's eyes. On one of the main streets, she came across a grand carriage, and inside it she spotted Erast. 'Oh!' Liza cried out, and then rushed towards him, but the carriage passed by and turned into a courtyard. Erast got out and was heading towards the porch of the large house, when he suddenly found himself... in Liza's arms. He turned pale, then without uttering a single word in response to her exclamation, he took her by the hand, led her into his study, locked the door, and said to her, 'Liza! Circumstances have changed. I am engaged to be married. You must leave me in peace and forget me for your own peace of mind. I loved you, and I still love you now: that is, I wish you well. Here are a hundred roubles. Take them.' He put the money in her pocket. 'Let me kiss you one last time, and then you must go home.'

Before Liza had chance to recover her senses, he had led her out of the study and instructed his servant to 'escort this girl out of the courtyard.'

At this point, my heart is bleeding. I am beginning to forget the human being inside Erast, and am ready to curse him, but my tongue will not move. I look up at the sky, and a tear rolls down my face. Oh, why am I writing this sad, true story, and not a novel?

So, had Erast deceived Liza by telling her that he was going away with the army? No, he really was in the army, but instead of fighting the enemy, he had played cards and gambled away almost all of his estate. Peace was soon declared, and Erast returned to Moscow, burdened with debt. There was only one way to improve his circumstances: to marry the rich, older widow who had been in love with him for a long time. He resolved to do that, and went to live in her house, heaving a genuine sigh for his Liza. But does all of that justify his actions?

Liza found herself on the street in such a state that no pen can describe. 'Has he spurned me? Does he love someone else? All is lost!' These were her thoughts and feelings! A severe fainting fit interrupted them temporarily. A kind woman who was passing by stopped and stood over Liza as she lay on the ground, and tried to revive her. The poor girl opened her eyes, and the kind woman helped her back onto her feet. Then she thanked the woman and walked on, not knowing where she was going. 'I cannot live,' thought Liza. 'I cannot! Oh, if only the sky would fall down on me! If only the earth would swallow me up, wretched as I am! Alas, the sky will not fall and the earth will not give way! Woe is me!'

She left the city and found herself at the edge of the deep pond, under the shade of those same ancient oaks which, a few weeks earlier, had been silent witnesses to her rapture. This memory shook her soul to the core; the most terrible, heartfelt suffering was evident on her face. For a few moments, though, she was lost in thought. She glanced around, spied her neighbour's daughter (a fifteen-year-old girl) walking along the road, and calling out to her, pulled the ten gold coins from her pocket, and gave them to the girl, saying, 'Anyuta, my dear friend! Take this money to my mother – it is not stolen – and tell her that Liza has sinned against her. Tell her that I concealed from her my love for a certain cruel man, E... Does she really need to know his name? Tell her that he betrayed me, and ask her to forgive me, God help her. Kiss her hand just as I am kissing yours now. Tell her that poor Liza told you to kiss her. Tell her that I...'

With that, she threw herself into the water. Anyuta screamed and burst into tears, but could not save her, so she ran to the village. A group of people gathered and pulled Liza out, but she was already dead.

Thus ended the life of one who was beautiful in body and soul. When we see each other in the next, new life, I will recognise you, sweet Liza!

She was buried near the pond, beneath that sombre oak, and a wooden cross was placed on her grave. I often sit there with my thoughts, leaning on the tomb where Liza is laid to rest, the pond rippling before my eyes, and the leaves rustling above me.

When Liza's mother heard of her daughter's terrible death, her blood ran cold and her eyes closed forever. The hut was left deserted. Inside it, the wind howls, and when the superstitious villagers hear the sound at night, they say, 'The dead girl is moaning. Poor Liza is moaning!'

Erast was unhappy for the rest of his days. When he learned of Liza's fate, he was inconsolable and considered himself a murderer. I met him a year before he died. He himself told me this story and took me to Liza's grave. Now, perhaps, they are reconciled at last!

The Nosegay
by Salomon Gessner
tr. George Baker, A.M.

'Twas she – 'twas Ida to the covert stray'd –
Would that I ne'er had seen the beauteous maid!
In fancy still her heavenly form I trace,
So lovely never seen, so full of grace.
Beneath a darkling willow stretch'd I lay,
What time the noontide pour'd its fiercest ray,
Breathing cool airs beside a brook that flow'd
With murmuring lapse along its pebbly road.
High waving shades o'ercanopied my head,
And o'er the bank and o'er the brook were spread;
A spot so tranquil seem'd for peace design'd –
But since that hour, alas! no peace I find.
'Twas then the rustling leaves a step betray'd,
And Ida softly glided through the shade.
Uplifting her light robe of azure hue,
Her slender snowy feet she bared to view;
Then stepp'd into the brook; with neck inclined
She stoop'd to meet the wave; one hand confined
Her falling vest, with the other from the pool
Pure draughts she raised her glowing cheek to cool.
Anon she paus'd—and from her fingers drain'd
The lingering lucid drops, till none remain'd;
And when the settled waves a mirror made
The conscious damsel smiled as she survey'd
Her charms unalter'd in the stream portray'd.

Then trimm'd her golden tresses that were twined
With studious art in one smooth knot behind.
'Ah then (I sigh'd) what means that bright attire,
What inward thoughts such wanton bliss inspire;
What favour'd youth is he, for whom she sees
Laughing those charms so confident to please?'
While Ida thus of matchless beauty proud
O'er the smooth lake her milk-white bosom bow'd,
It chanc'd the wild-flowers which but lately graced,
That milk-white bosom, carelessly displaced,
Dropp'd in the brook, and soon th' auspicious wave
Wafting, to me the precious trophy gave.
Gods! with what joy the blooming pledge I bore,
Kiss'd every tender flowret o'er and o'er,
Nor had a teeming herd of fattest kine
Bribed me, my fragrant fortune to resign.
But ah, since then scarce two brief days are flown,
Ere all their beauty fades, their scent is gone!
Alas, sad change – yet such a change is mine –
Like them my spirits droop, my hopes decline.
What boots it now that with a miser's hand
Secured, sweet flowers! within my cup ye stand,
(Proud cup, adjudg'd me by the shepherd throng
To crown the triumph of my spring-tide song.
There, aptly wrought with all the sculptor's power,
Lies Love, reposing in a wood-bine bower;
The god, with laughter lightening in his eyes,
Upon himself his arrowy mischief tries.
Near him, fit emblems of his gentle sway,

Two billing doves indulge their amorous play,)
Thrice every day refreshing draughts I bring,
To slake each thirsty stem, from clearest spring,
And every night, upon my window's brink,
Their closing bells ambrosial moisture drink.
In vain – upon their fading tints I bent
My steadfast gaze and caught their dying scent!
Once sweeter far than Maïa's sweetest bloom,
For Ida's bosom lent them rich perfume.
O Love, how dangerous is thine arrow found,
And I am doom'd to feel its deepest wound!
Oh may the beauteous maid be taught to share
But half the pangs which in my breast I bear –
Grant me this boon, propitious Deity,
And lo! this cup I consecrate to thee.
Upon an altar shall my offering rest,
And every morn with fragrant wreaths be dress'd.
Fresh flowers in summer shall the wreath compose,
And is it winter, still the myrtle blows,
Fair doves! may ye my future fate express,
Be ye the symbols of my love's success: –
Yet no – the flowers far other bodings give,
My hopes expire, for they refuse to live,
Sadly they droop, their closing cups are pale,
Their breath no longer feeds the passing gale! –
All-powerful Love be thou the shepherd's friend,
Let not these blighted flowers his blighted hope
portend.

The Stationmaster
by Alexander Sergeyevich Pushkin

Collegiate registrar[6],
Posting station dictator.

Prince Vyazemsky[7]

Who has never cursed stationmasters? Who has never quarrelled with them? Who, in a moment of rage, has not demanded they hand over that fateful book, in order to write in it a futile complaint of abuse, bad manners and sloppiness? Who does not consider them monsters in human form, equal to the unscrupulous clerks of old, or Murom's[8] robbers at least? We will, however, be fair and try to put ourselves in their position; then, perhaps, we might begin to judge them much more leniently. What exactly is a stationmaster? A real martyr of the

---

[6] Collegiate Registrar was classed as fourteen on the table of ranks (see below). (Translator's note)

[7] Prince Pyotr Andreyevich Vyazemsky was a Russian poet and friend of Alexander Pushkin. (Translator's note).

[8] A reference to fairy-tale hero, Ilya of Murom, who defended his country from robbers, monsters, and invaders. (Translator's note)

fourteenth rank[9], that rank protecting him only from beatings, and even then not always (I refer to the conscience of my readers). What is the duty of this kind of dictator, as Prince Vyazemsky calls him in jest? Is it not genuine hard labour? There is no peace to be had by day or by night. A traveller unburdens onto the stationmaster all the irritation accumulated during his tedious journey. Be it unpleasant weather, bad road conditions, a stubborn coachman or unobliging horses, the stationmaster is to blame. Upon entering the stationmaster's humble abode, a passing traveller sees him as an enemy; if he is able to rid himself of this uninvited guest quickly, then so much the better, but what if there are no horses? My goodness, what curses and threats will be showered upon him! He is forced to run from yard to yard in rain and slush, and in January's storms and hard frosts he might go out into the hallway just to get a moment's peace from the shouting and pushing of a disgruntled guest. If a general comes along, the trembling stationmaster will give him the last two troikas, including the one for the special courier. The general goes off without saying thank you. Five minutes later, a bell is heard... and the courier

---

[9] A reference to the Table of Ranks, first introduced by Peter the Great in an attempt to settle a struggle with the nobility. The ranks covered the military, civil service and the court, with the first being the highest, and the fourteenth the lowest. (Translator's note)

tosses his travel documents onto the table! Upon taking a closer look at all of this, our hearts will be filled not with indignation, but with genuine compassion. What is more, over the course of the twenty consecutive years that I have been travelling the length and breadth of Russia, I have come to know almost all of the posting routes. I am acquainted with several generations of coachmen, and rarely do I not recognise a stationmaster's face, those whom I have not encountered being few and far between. I hope to publish my curious collection of travel observations shortly, but in the meantime, I will merely say that the general opinion of stationmasters is quite wrong. These much-slandered people are essentially peace-loving, naturally obliging, sociably inclined, modest in their desire for praise, and not particularly avaricious. There are many interesting and informative things to be learned from their conversations (which gentlemen who are passing through unfortunately tend to avoid). For my part, I must admit, I prefer chatting with them than with some officious clerk of the sixth rank.

It is easy to guess that I have friends who belong to the honourable class of stationmasters. In fact, the memory of one of them is particularly precious to me. Circumstances brought us together once, and now I intend to tell my dear readers all about him.

In May 1816, I happened to be travelling through ***-skaya province, along a route that has since been decommissioned. I was low-ranking and travelling by stagecoach, having paid the fare for two horses. Consequently, the stationmasters did not stand on ceremony with me, and I often found myself fighting for what I believed to me mine by rights. Being young and hot-tempered, I would feel indignant at the stationmaster's meanness and pettiness when he harnessed the horses he had prepared for me onto some higher-ranking nobleman's carriage. For a long time, I could not get used to the fact that a fastidious servant would pass me by to serve a dish for some governor's dinner. Now it all seems quite normal to me. In fact, what would have become of us if, instead of the universally convenient rule of 'each according to his rank', a different rule were to be introduced, along the lines of 'each according to his mind'? What arguments would arise! And how would servants know whom to serve first? But I must return to my tale.

It was a hot day. Three versts[10] from *** station it started to drizzle, and a moment later torrential rain soaked me to the bone. Upon arriving at the posting station, my first concern was to change my clothes

---

[10] 1 verst = 1.1km or 0.66 mile. (Translator's note)

as quickly as possible, and my second was to order some tea.

'Hey, Dunya!' the stationmaster yelled. 'Put the samovar on and go fetch some cream.'

At these words, a girl of about fourteen emerged from behind a partition and ran into the hallway. I was stunned by her beauty.

'Is that your daughter?' I asked the stationmaster.

'Yes, Sir,' he replied, with an air of contented pride. 'She is intelligent and nimble, just like her late mother.'

With that, he set about copying down my travel details, while I examined the pictures that decorated his humble but neat and tidy home. They depicted the story of the Prodigal Son: on the first one, an elderly gentleman in a cap and dressing gown was bidding farewell to the restless youth who hastily accepted his blessing and a pouch full of money. In the next, the young man's dissolute behaviour was vividly portrayed: he was sitting at a table surrounded by false friends and shameless women. After that, having squandered everything, the young man, dressed in rags and a three-cornered hat, was feeding swine and sharing their meal, while his face expressed profound sorrow and remorse. Finally, there was an image of his return to his father: the kind old man, in the same cap and dressing gown, was running out to meet him; the prodigal son was kneeling; in the background, the cook was killing the fattened calf, and the older brother was questioning a servant about the reason for this celebration. Beneath each picture, I read the corresponding verses in German. It has all remained in my memory to this day, along with the pots of balsam, the bed with a multicoloured curtain, and the other objects that surrounded me at that moment. I can still see, as if it were now, my host himself, a man of about fifty who was fresh and cheery, and his long, green frock-coat with three medals on faded ribbons.

Before I had managed to pay my coachman what I owed, Dunya returned with the samovar. Seeing me now for the second time, the little coquette noticed the impression she had made on me, and lowered her big, blue eyes. I started talking to her, and she replied without the slightest timidity, like a girl who had seen the world. I offered her father a glass of punch, and I gave Dunya a cup of tea, then the three of us began to chat, as if we had known each other for ages.

The horses had been ready for a long time, but I was loath to part from the stationmaster and his daughter. Eventually, I bade them farewell. The father wished me a good journey, and the daughter accompanied me to the cart. In the hallway, I paused, and asked permission to kiss her. Dunya consented... I can count many more kisses

Since I first indulged in such things, back then,

but none has ever left me with such a lasting, delightful memory.

Several years passed, and circumstances led me down that same road, to that same place. I recalled the daughter of the old stationmaster, and was cheered by the thought of seeing her again. I did wonder, though, whether the old stationmaster might have been replaced, and Dunya was probably married by now. The thought that one or other of them might have died also flashed through my mind, and it was with a sad sense of foreboding that I approached *** station.

The horses came to a halt next to the posting station. Upon entering the room, I immediately recognised the pictures illustrating the story of the prodigal son; the table and bed were still in the same place, but there were no longer any flowers on the windowsills, and everything seemed worn out and neglected. The stationmaster was asleep, covered with an overcoat, but my arrival woke him, and he sat up... It was definitely Samson Vyrin, but how he had aged! While he was preparing to copy out my travel details, I looked at his grey hair, the deep wrinkles on his long-unshaven face, and his stooped back, and I could not help being surprised at how three or four years could turn such a sprightly person into a frail old man. 'Do you recognise me?' I asked him. 'We are old acquaintances.'

'Possibly,' he replied sullenly. 'This is a busy road. Lots of people have passed through here.'

'Is your Dunya in good health?' I went on.

The old man frowned. 'God knows,' he replied.

'Oh, so she is married, then?' I said.

The old man pretended not to hear my question and went on reading my travel papers in a whisper. I stopped asking questions and ordered some tea. Curiosity was starting to get the better of me and I hoped that some punch might loosen my old friend's tongue.

I was not mistaken: the old man did not refuse the glass I offered him. I noticed that the rum brightened up his dark mood. With the second glass, he became talkative, remembering me, or at least pretending that he did, and he told me a story that both beguiled me and moved me very much at the same time.

'So, you knew my Dunya, did you?' he began. 'Who didn't know her? Ah, Dunya! Dunya! What a girl she was! Everyone who came here would praise her, and no-one judged her. Ladies would give her scarves and earrings. Gentlemen travellers would linger here on purpose, supposedly to have lunch or dinner, but really just so that they could gaze at her for a while longer. No matter how angry a gentleman might be, he would calm down and talk politely with me when she was around. Believe me, Sir, couriers and special messengers could chat with her for half an hour at a time. She looked after the house: be it tidying or cooking, she managed to do it all. I, meanwhile, old fool that I am, couldn't get enough of looking at her and delighting in her. Didn't I love my Dunya after all, didn't I cherish my child, didn't she have a decent life? But no, you can't avoid trouble: whatever is meant to happen will happen.'

At this point he began to tell me in detail about his misfortune. Three years before, one winter's evening, the stationmaster had been ruling lines in a new book and his daughter was sewing herself a dress on the other side of the partition when a troika arrived and a traveller wearing a Circassian fur hat and a military greatcoat and wrapped in a shawl, entered the room, demanding horses. All the horses were out. When he heard this news, the traveller was about to raise his voice and his whip, but Dunya, who was quite accustomed to such situations, ran out from behind the partition and calmly asked the man if he would like something to eat. Dunya's appearance had its usual effect. The newcomer's anger vanished, he agreed to wait for the horses, and he ordered supper. After taking off his wet, shaggy fur hat, unwinding his shawl, and removing his coat, the traveller turned out to be a young, slender hussar with a black moustache. He settled himself down next to the stationmaster and began chatting merrily with him and his daughter. Supper was served. Meanwhile, the horses arrived and the stationmaster saw to it that they were harnessed up to the traveller's carriage straight away, without being fed. When he returned, though, he found the young man lying almost unconscious on the bench. He had been taken ill, his head was hurting, and he was not in a fit state to travel... What was to be done? The stationmaster gave him his own bed, and it was decided that if the patient felt no better the next day, they would send to S*** for a doctor.

The next day, the hussar was in a worse condition. His servant rode into the town to fetch a doctor. Dunya wound a kerchief soaked in vinegar around his head, and sat at his bedside with her sewing. Whenever the stationmaster was there the patient would groan and barely uttered a word, although he did drink two cups of coffee and, with a whimper, asked to be brought lunch. Dunya did not leave his side. He kept asking for something to drink, and Dunya brought him mugs of lemonade that she had made herself. The sick man would wet his lips, and each time he gave the mug back he would squeeze Dunya's hand with his own feeble one, as a gesture of thanks. The doctor arrived towards lunchtime. He felt the patient's pulse, spoke to him in German, then explained in Russian that all he needed was rest and that he would be able to travel again in a couple of days. The hussar paid him twenty-five roubles for the visit and invited him to stay to lunch. The doctor accepted the invitation, and they both ate with hearty appetites, consumed a bottle of wine, and parted on excellent terms.

A day later, the hussar was completely recovered. He was extremely happy, and constantly joking, sometimes with Dunya and sometimes with the stationmaster. He whistled songs, chatted with the travellers who were passing through, noted their travel details in the posting station book, and endeared himself to the good stationmaster to such an extent that on the third morning the host was sorry to part with such an amiable guest. It was a Sunday, and Dunya was getting ready to go to church. The hussar was given his carriage. He bade farewell to the stationmaster, rewarding him generously for the stay and the hospitality. He took his leave of Dunya, too, and offered to take her to church, as it was on the edge of the village.

Dunya was in a quandary...

'What are you afraid of?' asked her father. 'His excellency isn't a wolf, and he won't eat you: have a ride to church.'

Dunya climbed into the carriage next to the hussar, his servant leapt up onto the box, the coachman whistled, and the horses galloped away.

The poor stationmaster had no idea how he could have allowed his Dunya to go with the hussar, how he could have been so blind, and what could possibly have come over him. Before half an hour had passed, his heart had begun to ache and ache, and he was so uneasy that he could not stay put any longer, so he went to the church himself. As he approached, he saw that the congregation was already dispersing, but Dunya was neither in the grounds nor in the porch. He hurried inside the church: the priest was leaving the altar, the deacon was putting out the candles, and two old women were still praying in one corner, but Dunya was not there. The poor father promptly decided to ask the deacon whether she had been at the service. The deacon replied that she had not. Beside himself with worry, the stationmaster returned home. He had one last hope: some hairbrained youthful impulse might have led her to travel to the next staging post, where her godmother lived. He waited in agonising torment for the return of the troika in which he had sent her away. The coachman did not return. Eventually, towards evening, he arrived alone and inebriated, with the fateful news that, 'Dunya travelled on from that station with the hussar.'

The old man could not bear this misery and lay down at once on the very same bed where the young fraudster had lain the previous day. Now, as he thought about everything that had happened, he supposed that the illness must have been feigned. The poor stationmaster came down with a bad fever, he was taken to S***, and someone came to replace him for a while. The same doctor who had visited the hussar now treated him. He assured his patient that the young man had been quite well, and he had suspected his wicked intentions, but had remained silent for fear of his whip. Whether the German really was telling the truth, or whether he was just boasting about his far-sightedness, it was no consolation to his poor patient.

Scarcely had he recovered from his illness when the stationmaster asked the postmaster at S*** for two months' leave, and without telling anyone about his plans, he set out on foot to find his daughter. From his records, he knew that Cavalry Master Minsky had been travelling from Smolensk to St. Petersburg. The coachman who had driven him said that Dunya had cried all the way there, even though she seemed to be travelling of her own free will. 'Perhaps,' thought the stationmaster, 'I might be able to bring my lost sheep back home.' With this thought in mind, he arrived in St. Petersburg, staying in Izmailovsky Regiment, at the home of a retired non-commissioned officer, his old comrade-in-arms, and began his search. He soon learned that Cavalry Master Minsky was in St. Petersburg and staying at Demut's Inn. The stationmaster resolved to pay him a visit.

It was early in the morning when he arrived in the vestibule and requested a message to be sent to His Excellency that an old soldier wanted to meet with him. The valet, who was cleaning a boot on a block, stated that the master was sleeping and would not receive anyone before eleven o'clock. The stationmaster went away and returned at the appointed time. Minsky himself came out to meet him in a house-coat and a red cap.

'How can I help you, brother?' he asked.

The old man's heart began to race, his eyes welled up with tears, and all he could utter, in a quivering voice, was, 'Your excellency! Please grant me one blessed mercy!'

Minsky cast a swift glance at him, flushed, then took him by the arm and led him into his study and locked the door behind him.

'Your excellency!' the old man went on, 'Let bygones be bygones, but at least give me back my poor Dunya. You have had your fun now, so do not ruin her for nothing.'

'What is done cannot be undone,' the young man said, with the utmost discomfiture. 'I have wronged you and would like to beg your forgiveness. Do not assume, though, that I can give up Dunya: she will be happy, I give you my word. Why do you need her? She loves me, and she has moved on from her old life. Neither you nor she will forget what happened.' Then, tucking something into the fold of the old man's sleeve, he opened the door, and the stationmaster somehow found himself in the street outside.

He stood there, motionless, for a long time, until he finally noticed a bundle of papers in his sleeve. Pulling them out he unfolded several five- and ten-rouble notes. Once again, tears welled up in his eyes; tears of indignation! He crumpled the notes into a ball, tossed them onto the ground, stamped on them with his heel, and left... After walking a few paces, he stopped, thought for a moment... and went back... but the notes were no longer there. Spying him, a well-dressed young man ran up to a coachman, climbed hurriedly into his carriage, and shouted, 'Drive!' The stationmaster did not chase after him. He resolved to go back to his posting station, but before that, he wanted at least to see his poor Dunya one more time. To this end, he went to see Minsky a couple of days later, but the valet told him sternly that the master was not receiving anyone, then pushed him on the chest, shoving him out of the hallway, and slammed the door in his face. The stationmaster stood there for a long time, then went away.

In the evening of that same day, he was walking along Liteynaya Street, having attended prayers at the church of Our Lady Mother of all the Afflicted. Suddenly a fashionable drozhsky raced past in front of him, and the stationmaster recognised Minsky. The drozhsky pulled up directly in front of the entrance to a three-story building, and the hussar ran up to the porch. A happy thought entered the stationmaster's head. He turned back, and approaching the driver, asked him: 'Whose horse is this, brother? It wouldn't be Minsky's, would it?'

'It is indeed,' replied the driver. 'Why do you ask?'

'The thing is, your master told me to take a note to his Dunya, but I've gone and forgotten where she lives.'

'Here, on the second floor. But you are too late with your note, brother; he's here himself now.'

'Never mind,' the stationmaster told him, with an indescribable stirring in his heart. 'Thank you for the information, but I will complete my task all the same.' With these words, he went up the stairs.

The doors were locked, so he rang the bell, and several seconds passed in agonising anticipation. A key scraped in the lock and the door was opened in front of him.

'Is Avdotya Samsonovna here?' he asked.

'She is,' replied a young maid. 'What is your business with her?'

Without replying, the stationmaster walked into the hall.

'No, please don't!' the maid shouted after him. 'Avdotya Samsonovna has a visitor.'

Paying no attention, the stationmaster went further inside. The first two rooms were in darkness, but the third was lit up. He walked up to the open door and paused. Inside the room, which was beautifully furnished, Minsky was sitting, lost in thought. Dunya, dressed in the most luxurious fashion, was sitting on the arm of his chair, like a rider sitting side-saddle. She was gazing tenderly at Minsky and winding his black curls around her sparkling fingers. The poor stationmaster! Never had his daughter seemed so beautiful, and he could not help admiring her.

'Who is there?' she asked, without looking up. He said nothing. Having received no reply, Dunya raised her head... and, letting out a scream, collapsed onto the rug. In fright, Minsky rushed to help her up, but seeing the old stationmaster standing in the doorway, he left Dunya and walked towards him, shaking with rage.

'What do you want?' he said through clenched teeth. 'What are you doing, creeping in here like a robber? Or are you planning to kill me? Get out!' Then, his strong hand grabbing the old man by the collar, he pushed him out onto the staircase.

The old man went back to his own lodgings. His friend advised him to file a complaint, but the stationmaster thought for a moment, then waved his hand and decided to leave the matter alone. Two days later, he left St. Petersburg for his posting station, and resumed his duties. 'For three years, now,' he concluded, 'I have been living without Dunya, with neither sight nor sound of her. God knows whether she is alive or not. These things happen. She is not the first and will not be the last to be lured away by some rake, to be held onto for a while and then abandoned. There are plenty such young fools in St. Petersburg, dressed in satin and velvet today, and tomorrow sweeping the streets with beggars. Sometimes it makes you wonder whether Dunya might end up that way, and then you find yourself sinning by wishing that she might die...'

That was the story of my acquaintance, the old stationmaster; a story that was interrupted many times by tears, which he wiped away emotively with the edge of his jacket, like the earnest Terentych in Ivan Dmitriev's beautiful ballad, 'The Caricature'. These tears were partly induced by the punch, as he had made his way through five glasses of the stuff over the course of his storytelling, but my heart was, nevertheless, still profoundly moved by them. When we parted, I could not get the old stationmaster out of my head for a long time, and I thought about his Dunya a lot...

Recently, when I was passing through ***, I recalled my acquaintance, and learned that the posting station where he worked had been closed down. When I asked, 'Is the old stationmaster still alive?' no-one could give me a satisfactory answer. I decided to pay a visit to that familiar place, so I hired what horses were available and set off for the village of N.

This took place in autumn. Grey clouds covered the sky, a cold wind was blowing over the harvested fields, carrying along the red and yellow leaves from the occasional trees. I arrived in the village at sunset and stopped by the posting house. From out of the hallway (where poor Dunya had once kissed me) appeared a portly woman who, in answer to my questions, said that the old stationmaster had died a year or so ago, and that a brewer had moved into the cottage, and she was the wife of that brewer. I felt sorry that my trip had been wasted, and regretted the seven roubles that it had cost.

'What did he die of?' I asked the brewer's wife.

'He drank himself to death, sir,' she replied.

'Where is he buried?'

'On the outskirts of the village, next to his dead missus.'

'I don't suppose someone could take me to his grave?'

'Why not? Hey, Vanka! Stop messing about with that cat. Take this gentleman to the cemetery and show him the stationmaster's grave.'

At these words, a boy in ragged clothes, red-haired and squint-eyed, ran out to me and took me straight to the outskirts of the village.

'Did you know the man?' I asked him on the way.

'How could I not know him! He taught me to carve wooden flutes. He used to come out of the tavern (God rest his soul!) and we would follow him, shouting, 'Mister, mister! Nuts!' Then he would give us hazelnuts. He was always playing around with us.'

'Do travellers remember him?'

'There aren't many travellers now, unless the assessor turns up, but he's not interested in the dead.

In the summer a lady came; she asked about the old stationmaster and went to his grave.'

'What was the lady like?' I asked, curious.

'A fine lady,' replied the boy. 'She was travelling in a carriage with six horses, three small children, a nurse and a black pug. When she was told that the old stationmaster had died, she burst into tears and told her children, 'Sit nicely while I go to the cemetery.' So, I volunteered to take her. But the lady said, 'I know the way.' Then she gave me a five-kopek coin. She was such a kind lady!'

We arrived at the cemetery: it was a bleak place that was not defined by any kind of boundary. It was dotted with wooden crosses, but there was not a single tree to provide shade. I had never seen such a sorry-looking graveyard.

'This is the old stationmaster's grave,' the boy told me, leaping onto a sandy mound, stuck into which was a black cross with a copper icon.

'Did the lady come here?' I asked.

'She did. I watched her from a distance. She lay down here, and for a long time, too. Then she went into the village, asked for the priest, gave him some money, and went away. She gave me a silver five-kopek coin, as well. A nice lady!'

I, too, gave the boy a five-kopek coin and no longer regretted my trip or the seven roubles I had spent on it.

Eternal Memory
by Helen Hagon

Beside the mournful Moskva river,
an oak bears witness for ages to come.
A grove where birch trees with memories shiver,
of rapturous devotion and innocence undone.

A grave wherein is laid to rest
the purest love that hoped in vain.
A soul who gave her very best,
but in return received only pain.

Fairer than flowers, heaven's lovely daughter,
fresher than new petals unfurled,
more faithful than the Moskva's waters:
too perfect for this tainted world.

In heartfelt lines inscribed with care,
her memory lives on each page we turn.
Therein is stored a treasure most rare,
thus preserved that we might learn.

The Graveyard
by Nikolai Mikhailovich Karamzin

First voice

It is terrible in the cold, dark grave!
Here the winds howl, the coffins shake,
white bones rattle.

Second voice

All is quiet in the soft and peaceful grave.
Here the breezes blow, cooling those who sleep;
grass and flowers abound.

First

The bloodthirsty worm gnaws away at the deceased;
in yellowing skulls toads make their nests;
snakes hiss among the nettles.

Second

Deep, sweet and mild is the sleep of the dead;
inside the coffin there is no storm;
birds sing over the grave.

First

Black ravens dwell in this place;
those avaricious birds, beasts of prey,
clamour and peck at the ground.

Second

In the green grass, a little rabbit
rests with his dear little sweetheart.
A dove sleeps on a branch.

First

Dampness and gloom, tightly mingled,
float there, in the stifling air.
A tree stands, leafless.

Second

There, streaming through the clear air,
is the sweet fragrance of blue violets,
white jasmine and lilies.

First

The wanderer fears the valley of death,
his heart filled with terror and awe.
Past the graveyard he hastens.

Second

The weary wanderer spies the dwelling place
of eternal peace, and throwing his stick away,
remains there forever.

Part 3: The Stranger in Gravesend

Although many of Karamzin's now-familiar stylistic elements are present in our next story, *Bornholm Island*, it is quite distinct from his earlier sentimental tales. Here, the narrator is a fully-fledged character, retelling the events of his sea voyage from England back home to Russia, with a stopover on the Danish island of Bornholm. The story opens in England where, whilst waiting for appropriate weather for the trip, the narrator meets a tormented stranger with a guitar, who is also far from home, and who proceeds to sing of his woes in his native Danish. The song itself cryptically foreshadows the rest of the story, in which the narrator explores the mysterious Bornholm Island with its Gothic castle and strange inhabitants, and uncovers a terrible secret.

As in Karamzin's previous tales, the setting is used to reflect the action, but here this means harsh rock faces, darkness, turbulent seas and cold temperatures, instead of flower-strewn meadows and beautiful birdsong. There is also a love story, but this time it is shrouded in mystery and left to the reader to surmise. The theme of travel recalls Karamzin's earlier work, *Letters of a Russian*

Traveller, and was perhaps inspired by his extensive travels around Europe.

Here, as in *Eugene and Julia*, there are also subtle allusions to incest, and we will see this again later in *A Knight of our Time*. The song mentions that the love of the singer's life has been banished 'by the oath of a scrupulous parent', and although nothing is made explicit, the reader cannot help but wonder about the identity of the girl in the dungeon and the nature of the 'dreadful secret'.

Bornholm Island is followed by an extract from *A Hero of our Time* by M.Yu. Lermontov (1814-1841), another much-loved Russian poet and writer who would have been familiar with Karamzin's work. This particular scene is strikingly similar to the encounter with the stranger at Gravesend. Here, too, there is a mysterious singer, this time a girl, and her mermaid-like song also seems to possess some kind of hidden meaning, if not magical power. Finally, given that Lermontov reportedly penned his poem *Clouds* while at Karamzin's house, it would be a shame not to include this to round off the chapter.

Bornholm Island
by Nikolai Mikhailovich Karamzin

Friends! The beautiful summer has passed by, golden autumn has turned pale, the greenery has withered, trees stand without fruit or leaves, the misty sky is turbulent like a dark sea, and winter is sprinkling its down over the cold earth: let us bid farewell to nature until our joyful reunion in the spring, and let us shelter from blizzards and snowstorms, ensconced in our own quiet studies! Time must not weigh us down – we know a cure for tedium. Friends! Oak and birch logs burn in our hearths – let the winds rage and cover our windows with white snow! Let us sit around the bright red fire and tell each other tales, stories and all kinds of yarns.

As you know, I have roamed around foreign lands, far away from my homeland, far from you who are so dear to my heart. I have seen many wonderful things, and heard much that surprised me, and I have told you a great deal, but I cannot recount every single thing that has happened to me. Listen, and I will tell you a story – a true story, not a work of fiction.

England was the furthest extent of my travels. While I was there, I told myself, 'Your homeland and your friends are waiting for you; it is time to settle down in their embrace, time to dedicate your traveller's staff to the son of Maia[11], time to bear it to the thickest branch of the tree beneath which you played in your younger years.' Having said this, I boarded a ship called *Britannia* in London, ready to sail to my beloved land of Russia.

We sped swiftly beneath white sails, along the flower-covered banks of the majestic river Thames. The endless blue expanse of the sea was already stretching out before us, and we could hear its tumultuous sound when the wind suddenly changed, and our ship, which had been expecting favourable weather conditions, was obliged to dock near a place called Gravesend.

The captain and I went ashore, and I strolled with a peaceful heart through green meadows adorned by nature and hard work, and over occasional picturesque bridges. Eventually, exhausted by the heat of the sun, I lay down on the grass beneath a centuries-old elm tree not far from the seashore, and gazed at the watery expanse and the billowing foam whose countless ranks rushed forth, one after another, out of the gloomy distance and towards the island, letting out a muffled roar. This desolate

---

[11] In antiquity, it was customary for travellers to dedicate their staffs to Mercury, the son of Maia, upon returning to their homeland.

sound, along with the view across the never-ending waters, began to lull me into a slumber and to that sweet idleness of the soul wherein all thoughts and feelings come to a standstill, like streams suddenly freezing over, and which presents the most striking and poetic image of death; but then the branches above my head suddenly began to shake... I looked up and saw a young man. He was gaunt, pale and languid; more of a ghost than a person. He was holding a guitar in one hand, and tearing leaves from the tree with the other, whilst gazing at the blue sea with his unmoving, dark eyes wherein shone the last glimmer of an expiring life. I was unable to look him in the eye, since his senses were dead to external things: he was standing two paces away from me, but he heard and saw nothing. 'Poor young man!' I thought. 'You have been smitten by fate. I know neither your name nor your provenance, but I do know that you are unhappy!'

He sighed and looked up at the sky, then back down at the waves on the sea. Walking away from the tree, he sat on the grass, and began to play a sad refrain on his guitar, whilst staring at the sea. Then he started to sing along in a soft voice (in the Danish language, which my acquaintance, Doctor N., taught me when I was in Geneva):

*Laws may have judged and condemned
the object of my affection;
but who, dear heart, can withstand
your loving determination?*

*What law is more sacred and inviolable
than your natural sensitivity?
What power is stronger and more unshakeable
than instinctive love and beauty?*

*I love and will love endlessly.
Curse my innocent passion,
ye ruthless souls without mercy,
cruel hearts without compassion!*

*Sacred Nature, hear this cry
from your dear son and friend,
who, innocent before you, lies.
To me this heart you did send:*

*in your goodness you adorned her
with your gifts most precious and rare.
You willed me to fall in love, oh Nature,
with Lila so beautiful and fair!*

*Your thunder shook the sky above,
but we were safe from harm,*

> *locked in the tender embrace of love,*
> *delighting in its charm.*
>
> *O Bornholm, dear Bornholm!*
> *My soul for you doth yearn,*
> *never resting, wherever I may roam,*
> *and yet I weep in vain.*
>
> *Here I languish and lament,*
> *now banished from your shores*
> *by the oath of a scrupulous parent,*
> *to sigh forever more!*
>
> *Are you still there, my dearest Lila?*
> *Are you living in anguish and strife?*
> *Or have you entered the crashing waters*
> *and put an end to your cruel life?*
>
> *Appear to me, gracious apparition:*
> *to behold you again I crave!*
> *I will be your watery companion*
> *in the billowing, raging waves.*

At that point, an involuntary stirring within made me want to rush over to the stranger and put my arms around him, but at that very moment, my captain took me by the hand and informed me that a favourable wind was filling our sails, and there was no time to lose... We set sail. The young man, arms folded and guitar tossed aside, watched us departing, and gazed at the blue sea...

The waves foamed beneath the helm of our ship, the shore at Gravesend disappeared into the distance, the northern provinces of England darkened on the other extreme of the horizon... and eventually everything vanished, while the birds, who had been hovering above us for a long time, flew back towards the shore, as if frightened by the vastness of the sea. The noisy, churning waters and the fog-bound sky were the only objects we could set eyes on: objects that were both majestic and terrifying... My friends, in order to vividly appreciate the full audacity of the human spirit, you have to be on the open sea, where 'one slender plank of wood', as Wieland says, 'separates us from a watery death', but where a skilled sailor can glide along, having let out his sails, and in his thoughts he can already see the glimmer of gold with which his courageous endeavours will be rewarded in another part of the world. 'Nil mortalibus arduum est,' (Nothing is impossible to mortals), I thought, along with Horace, my gaze lost in the infinity of Neptune's realm.

Soon, however, a vicious attack of seasickness deprived me of my senses. For six days my eyes did not open and my languorous heart, showered with foam[12] from the stormy waves, could barely bring itself to beat inside my chest. On the seventh day, I came round, and with a pale but happy face, I went out on deck. The sun, in the pure azure vault, had already moved westwards, and illuminated by its golden rays, the sea roared, while the ship glided along at full sail, over the rolling swell which sought in vain to overwhelm our vessel. All around us, at various distances away, fluttered white, blue and pink flags, and to my right was something black which resembled land.

'Where are we?' I asked the captain.

'Our voyage has gone smoothly,' he said. 'We have passed the Sound, and the shores of Sweden are just out of sight. To your right you can see the Danish Island of Bornholm, a perilous place for ships, as there are shallows and hidden rocks on the seabed. When night falls we will drop anchor.'

'Bornholm Island! Bornholm Island!' I kept repeating in my head, and the image of the young stranger at Gravesend came to mind. The mournful strains and the words of his song rang in my ears. 'His heart's secret is locked within them,' I thought. 'But who *is* he? Which laws could have condemned

---

[12] I really was showered with foam from the waves as I lay unconscious on deck.

this poor man's love? What kind of oath banished him from the shores of Bornholm which were so dear to him? Will I ever learn his story?'

Meanwhile, a strong wind bore us straight towards the island. Its ominous cliffs had already come into view, and from them raging, foaming torrents seethed forth and plunged into the sea. It appeared to be impregnable from all sides, as if secured by the hand of majestic nature, and I could imagine nothing that was not terrible beyond that grey rock face. Awestruck, I saw there the image of cold, silent eternity, of inexorable death, and of that ineffable creative power before which every mortal should tremble.

The sun sank into the waves, and we dropped anchor. The wind died down and there was barely a ripple on the sea. I looked at the island which was beckoning me to its shores by means of some inexplicable force, and a dark sense of foreboding told me, 'You can satisfy your curiosity there, and Bornholm will remain in your memory forever!' Eventually, having discovered that there were some fishermen's huts near the shore, I decided to ask the captain for a boat and go onto the island with two or three sailors. He warned me about the dangers, and about the underwater rocks, but seeing the determination of his passenger, he agreed to my request on condition that I return to the ship early the following morning.

We set out and arrived safely on shore in a small, quiet cove. We were greeted there by some sailors; coarse, wild people who had grown up accustomed to the cold elements and the noise of the rolling waves, and who knew not how to greet with a friendly smile. For all that, though, they were neither cunning nor wicked people. Upon hearing that we wanted to take a look at the island and spend the night in their huts, they tied up our boat and led us through a crumbling, rocky mountain of flint, towards their homes. After half an hour, we emerged onto a vast green plain strewn with low wooden cottages, copses and heaps of stones. I left my sailors there, and went on further by myself, to enjoy the delights of the evening for a little longer. A boy of about thirteen was my guide.

The scarlet hue of sunset had not yet faded in the bright sky, its rosy glow falling on the white granite rocks, and in the distance, beyond a large hill, it lit up the pointed towers of an ancient castle. The boy could not tell me to whom the castle belonged. 'We do not venture there,' he said. 'And God only knows what goes on inside!' I redoubled my steps and soon neared the huge, gothic building surrounded by a deep moat and a high wall. Silence reigned all around, the sea could be heard far away, and the last ray of evening light was dwindling above the bronze spires on top of the towers.

I walked around the castle: the gates were closed and the drawbridge raised. My guide, although he himself did not know why, was afraid and begged me to go back to the huts, but how could a curious person agree to such a request?

Night had fallen when a voice suddenly called out: an echo repeated it, and then all was silent again. Terrified, the boy grabbed me by both hands, trembling like a condemned man before his execution. A minute later, the voice sounded again. It asked, 'Who is there?'

'A stranger from a foreign land,' I said, 'brought to this island by his curiosity, and if hospitality is considered a virtue within the walls of your castle, then pray open up for this wanderer in the dark hours of the night.' There was no reply, but a few minutes later, the drawbridge began to rumble as it was lowered from the tower, and the gates opened noisily. A tall man in a long, black robe came out to meet me, took me by the arm, and led me into the castle. I looked back, but the boy who had come with me had made himself scarce.

The gates banged shut behind us, while the bridge rumbled again as it was hoisted back up. We walked across a spacious courtyard overgrown with shrubs, nettles and wormwood, and arrived at a large house, in which a lamp was burning. A high peristyle, after the classical fashion, led to an iron portico whose steps rang beneath our feet. All around was darkness and emptiness. In the first hall, encircled on the inside by a gothic colonnade, hung a lantern, the pale light from which only just managed to reach the rows of gilded pillars that were crumbling with age: in one place lay pieces of a cornice, in another were fragments of pilasters, and in a third were entire fallen columns. Several times, my guide glanced at me with piercing eyes, but he did not utter a single word.

All of this created a strange impression in my heart; a mixture of terror and a mysterious, inexplicable delight which might be better expressed as a pleasant anticipation of something extraordinary.

We passed through a further two or three lamplit halls which were similar to the first one. Then a door opened to our right: in the corner of a small room sat a distinguished-looking, grey-haired old gentleman, his elbows leaning on a table whereupon two white wax candles were burning. He raised his head, looked at me with a kind of mournful tenderness, offered me his frail hand, and said in a soft, pleasant voice, 'Although eternal sorrow dwells within the walls of this castle, a traveller requesting hospitality will always find a peaceful refuge herein. Stranger! I do not know you, but you are a person, and my dying heart is still alive with love for people, so my house and my arms are open to you in welcome.' He embraced me and gave me a seat, and his efforts to cheer up his gloomy expression made him resemble one of those clear but chilly autumn days which are more reminiscent of doleful winter than joyful summer. He wanted to be welcoming, but with his smile he also wanted to assure me that the sorrows deep within his face could not be dispelled in a mere instant.

'Young man, you must...' he said, 'you must tell me about all the happenings in the world which I have abandoned but not altogether forgotten. For a long time I have lived in solitude, and for a long time I have heard nothing of how people have been faring. Tell me, does love prevail around the globe? Does incense burn on the altars of virtue? Do people prosper in the countries you have seen?'

'The enlightenment of learning,' I replied, 'is spreading more and more, but human blood is still being spilled onto the ground, the unfortunate are shedding tears, and virtue is praised while its existence is disputed.'

The old man sighed and shrugged his shoulders. Upon learning that I was a Russian, he said, 'We originate from the same people as you. The ancient inhabitants of the islands of Rügen and Bornholm were Slavs. But the light of Christianity shone upon you first. Magnificent cathedrals dedicated to the one God already towered up to the clouds in your country while we were still dwelling in the darkness of idolatry and making bloody sacrifices to inanimate graven images. You were already singing triumphant hymns of praise to the great creator of the universe, while we, blinded by delusion, were praising mythical idols in discordant songs.' The old man talked with me about the history of the northern peoples, bygone antiquity and modern times. He spoke in such a way that I could not help but marvel at his mind, his knowledge, and even his eloquence.

Half an hour later he rose and bade me a good night. Taking a candle from the table, the servant in the black robe led me through long narrow passages, until we arrived at a large room in which were hung ancient weapons, swords, spears, armour and helmets. In a corner, beneath a golden canopy, stood a high bed decorated with carvings and ancient bas-reliefs.

I wanted to ask this man a multitude of questions, but before I could voice them, he bowed and left. The iron door banged shut, the sound ringing ominously around the empty walls, then all was quiet. I lay on the bed, looked at the antique weapons illuminated by a feeble beam of moonlight coming through the tiny window, and thought about my host and the first words he had said to me: 'Eternal sorrow dwells within the walls of this castle.'

I wondered about times past, and about those adventures which this ancient castle had witnessed. I wondered, like a person gazing upon the remains of the dead among coffins and graves and bringing them to life in his imagination. Eventually, the image of the sad stranger in Gravesend came to mind; then I fell asleep.

My sleep was not peaceful, though. It seemed to me that all the suits of armour on the wall had turned into knights, and that these knights were advancing on me with unsheathed swords and angry faces, saying, 'Miserable wretch! How dare you come to our island? Do sailors not pale at the sight of our granite shores? How dare you enter the dreaded sanctuary of the castle? Do its horrors not resound all about? Do travellers not keep their distance from its fearsome towers? Impudent rogue! You must die for this egregious curiosity!'

Swords clattered above me and blows rained down onto my chest, but then everything disappeared in an instant. I woke up, but a minute later I was asleep again. At once my spirit was troubled by a new dream. Terrible thunder seemed to be rumbling inside the castle, the iron doors were banging, the windows shaking, the floor swaying, and a fearsome winged monster which I cannot describe flew at my bed with a roar and a screech. The dream vanished, but I still could not sleep and, feeling in need of fresh air, I went over to the window. Beside it I discovered a small door, so I opened it and descended a steep flight of stairs into the garden.

The night was clear, and the light of the full moon turned dark green to silver on the ancient oaks and elms which formed a dense, long avenue. The swishing of the waves on the sea joined with the rustling of the leaves shaken by the wind. In the distance were the white, craggy mountains which surround Bornholm Island like battlements; between these and the walls of the castle, a large forest could be seen on one side, while on the other was an open plain with small clusters of trees.

My heart was still pounding from the terrifying dreams, and my blood had not stopped rushing. I stepped into the dark avenue, beneath the canopy of rustling oaks, and with a certain reverence, plunged into its shadows. The thought of druids entered my head, and it seemed to me that I was approaching that sacred place where all the mysteries and horrors of their religion were kept. Eventually the long avenue brought me to some rosemary bushes, beyond which rose a sandy hill. I was about to climb to the top of it, to gaze at the view of the sea and the island in the bright moonlight, but then an entrance in the hillside appeared before my eyes: it was just possible for a person to fit through it. Irresistible curiosity drew me into the cave, which seemed more like the work of human hands than a product of wild nature. I went inside, felt the dampness and the cold, but resolved to go further, and after moving ten or so paces forwards, I noticed some steps going down and a wide iron door which, to my surprise, was not locked. My hand seemed to open it automatically: there, beyond an iron grille, on which hung a large padlock, shone a lamp attached to an arch, and in the corner, on a bed of straw, lay a pale young woman in a black dress. She was sleeping. Her fair hair, into which yellow strands of straw had woven themselves, covered her high chest, which was scarcely breathing, and one white but withered hand lay on the ground, while the head of the sleeping woman rested on the other. If a painter had wanted to portray languid, endless, perpetual sorrow strewn with the poppies of Morpheus, then this woman could have served as the perfect model for his brush.

My friends, who would not be moved by the sight of someone so unfortunate! But the sight of this young woman suffering in an underground prison – the sight of the weakest and most gracious of creatures oppressed by fate – would fill even a stone with emotion. Grief-stricken, I watched her and thought to myself, 'What barbaric hand has deprived you of daylight? Have you really committed such a terrible crime? Yet your pretty face, the gentle movement of your chest, and my own heart assure me of your innocence!'

At that very minute she woke up... glanced at the grille... noticed me... was surprised... lifted her head... rose... came closer... lowered her eyes, as if gathering her thoughts... then stared at me again, and was about to say something, but did not.

'If the sensitivity of a traveller,' I said after a few moments' silence, 'who was brought to this castle and this cave by the hand of destiny, could ease your burden, and if his genuine compassion is worthy of your trust, then ask for his help!'

She looked at me with unmoving eyes, in which I perceived surprise, a certain curiosity, indecision and doubt. Finally, something powerful stirred within her, shaking her chest like an electric shock, and she replied firmly, 'Whoever you may be, and whatever circumstances may have brought you here, stranger, I cannot ask anything of you except pity. You have no power to change my destiny. I kiss the hand that punishes me.'

'But is your heart not innocent?' I said. 'Surely it does not deserve such a cruel punishment!'

'My heart,' she replied, 'may have erred. God will pardon the weak. I hope that my life will end soon. Leave me, stranger!'

At that, she approached the grille, looked at me with tenderness, and repeated in hushed tones, 'For God's sake, leave me! If it was he who sent you – the one whose dreadful curse forever rings in my ears – then tell him that I am suffering, that I suffer day and night, that grief has withered my heart, and that tears no longer relieve my anguish. Tell him that I will endure my imprisonment without grumbling and without complaint, and that I will die his gentle, unfortunate…'

She suddenly fell silent, thought for a moment, and moved away from the bars. Kneeling down, she covered her face with her hands. A moment later, she glanced at me, then lowered her eyes again, saying with gentle timidity, 'It may be that you know my story, but if not, then do not ask me about it. For God's sake, do not ask! Forgive me, stranger!'

I said a few words to her, pouring them straight from my soul, and was about to leave, but my eyes met hers again, and it seemed to me that she wanted to ask me about something that was important to her heart. I stopped and waited for the question to come, but after a heavy sigh, it died on her pale lips. We parted.

Upon leaving the cave, I refrained from closing the iron door, so that the fresh, pure air could flow through the grille and into the darkness, allowing the poor girl to breathe more easily. Dawn had turned the sky scarlet, the birds were waking up, and a breeze was blowing the dew from the bushes and flowers that grew around the sandy hill.

'My God!' I thought. 'My God! How sad it is to be excluded from the company of the living, free, happy creatures that inhabit nature's spaces everywhere! In the far north, among tall, moss-covered rocks, formidable to behold, your creation is beautiful: the work of your hand delights the heart and spirit. Even here, where foamy waves have battled with the granite cliffs since the beginning of the world. Here, where your right hand imprinted the living signs of a creator's love and goodness. Here, where in the morning hour, roses bloom against the azure sky. Here, where gentle Zephyrs[13] are filled with fragrances. Here, where green carpets spread out like soft velvet beneath a person's feet. Here, where the birds sing happily for the happy, and sorrowfully for the sorrowful, pleasing everyone. Here, where a grieving heart might find relief from the burden of its woes in the embrace of sensitive nature! However, that poor captive in her dungeon has none of this comfort: her languishing heart is not sprinkled with the morning dew, the breeze does not refresh her withered breast, the sun's rays do not light up her darkened eyes, and the moon's quiet, soothing effusions do not feed her soul with gentle dreams and pleasant thoughts. Creator! Why did

---

[13] A light breeze. Named after Zephyr, the Greek god of the west wind. (Translator's note)

you grant people the fatal power to make each other and themselves unhappy?'

My strength was gone, and my eyes closed beneath the soft greenery on the branches of a tall oak tree.

I continued to sleep for about two hours.

'The door was open. The foreigner has been into the cave.'

This was what I heard as I awoke, opening my eyes to behold my elderly host. He was sitting, lost in thought, on a turf seat, about five steps away from me, and standing next to him was the same man who had brought me into the castle. I walked towards them. The old man gave me a rather stern glance, then stood up and shook my hand, whereupon his expression became kinder. Together, we walked into a densely wooded avenue, without uttering a word. His soul seemed to be hesitating and undecided, but then he suddenly stopped, and staring at me with piercing, burning eyes, he asked in a firm voice: 'Did you see her?'

'I did,' I replied. 'I saw her, but I did not discover who she is and why she is suffering in a prison.'

'You shall discover,' he said. 'You shall discover, young man, and your heart will bleed. Then you will ask yourself why heaven poured out a whole portion of its wrath upon this frail, grey-haired old man; an old man who has loved virtue, and who has respected heaven's holy laws.'

We sat down beneath a tree, and the old man told me the most terrible story; a story which you shall not hear now, my friends. It will remain for another time. For now, I shall merely tell you that I learned the secret of the stranger in Gravesend: a dreadful secret!

The sailors were waiting for me at the castle gates. We returned to the ship, raised the sails, and Bornholm disappeared out of sight.

The sea roared. In my grief-stricken reverie, I stood on deck, my hand gripping the mast. My chest was wracked with sighs. Eventually I glanced at the sky and the wind blew my tear into the sea.

Extract from 'A Hero of Our Time'
by Mikhail Yuriyevich Lermontov

I wrapped myself up in my cloak and sat down on a rock by the fence, gazing into the distance. An agitated sea stretched out before me, like a storm in the night, and its monotonous sound, which resembled the murmur of a city falling asleep, reminded me of years gone by, transporting my thoughts to the north and our cold capital. Stirred by my memories, I lost track of time... An hour must have passed in that way, possibly more... Suddenly, my ears caught the strains of something that sounded like a song. It was indeed a song, sung by a fresh, female voice, but where was it coming from? I listened carefully. The melody was strange, being drawn-out and melancholy, yet brisk and lively. I glanced around, but there was no-one nearby. I listened again. The sounds seemed to be falling from the sky. I looked up and, standing on the roof of my hut, was a girl in a striped dress, with her hair hanging loose: a true mermaid. Her hand shielding her eyes from the sun, she was staring into the distance, laughing and talking to herself, and from time to time launching into another refrain.

I remember this song word for word:

> *As if set free,*
> *all the ships sail by,*
> *across the green sea*
> *with white sails raised high.*
> *My little boat trails*
> *in the midst of these vessels.*
> *A boat without sails,*
> *but with two wooden paddles.*
> *When a storm is raging,*
> *these old sailing ships*
> *will lift their wings*
> *and over the sea will slip.*
> *To the sea I will bow down*
> *and softly say:*
> *'Wicked sea, do not harm*
> *my little boat today.*
> *My little boat carries along*
> *a cargo rare and precious.*
> *A soul, bold and headstrong,*
> *guides her through the darkness.'*

It occurred to me that I had heard that same voice during the night. I thought for a moment, and when I looked up at the roof again, the girl was not there. Suddenly, she ran past me, humming something else, and clicking her fingers, ran up to an old woman, whereupon they started to argue. The old woman was angry and the girl laughed loudly. Then

I spotted my little Undine skipping along again. She came towards me, stopped, and stared at me, as if surprised by my presence. Nevertheless, she turned away nonchalantly and strolled quietly over to the pier. But that was not the end of it: she whirled about past my lodgings all day long, and her singing and leaping did not cease for a minute. What a strange creature! Her face revealed no signs of madness: on the contrary, she fixed me with a bold, penetrating glare, from eyes endowed with some kind of magnetic power, and every time they seemed to be waiting for a question. Whenever I began to speak, though, she ran off, grinning mischievously.

Clouds
by Mikhail Yuriyevich Lermontov

Heavenly clouds, eternal vagabonds!
Across the azure steppe, like a string of pearls,
as if exiles like me, you scud along
from north to south, around the world.

Who is driving you: fate or decision?
Some secret envy? Blatant anger?
Are you weighed down by some transgression?
Or by friends' malicious slander?

No! Barren fields are all you see...
Passions and sufferings to you are unknown;
forever cold, forever free,
you are no exile if you have no home.

The Shore
by Nikolai Mikhailovich Karamzin

After raging storm and surging waters,
and all the dangers that may befall,
when entering the peaceful harbour
sailors know no doubt at all.

Be it utterly unknown!
Be it not on any map or chart!
By the bewitching hope they are drawn
that all their troubles may there depart.

If upon the shore they spy
a friend or other familiar face,
'Oh, such happiness!' they will cry
and fly at once into their embrace.

Life! You are the sea and the raging waters!
Death! You are the harbour of tranquility.
May those here by a wave torn asunder
be reunited there for eternity.

You are beckoning us, I realise,
to hasten towards your mysterious shores!
Save a place at your side,
dear shadows, for these friends of yours!

Part 4: An Unlikely Knight

The final Karamzin story in this selection is perhaps the most complex and was certainly the trickiest to translate. *A Knight of Our Time* is an account of the childhood of a boy called Leon. His beloved mother dies, but a countess, who has recently retired to the country, offers to take charge of his education and become a 'second mama' to him. However, the nature of this education, combined with Leon's fondness for reading novels, and the increasing intimacy of his relationship with the countess, lead to an episode which is deliberately modelled on the story of Diana and Actaeon, as told in Ovid's *Metamorphoses*.

This work represents a new phase in Karamzin's style, as there is an obvious element of parody, poking fun at his own and others' Sentimentalist writing, almost as if he is rounding off his Sentimentalist phase, in preparation for settling down to the more serious business of working on his *History of the Russian State*.

I have taken a few more liberties with the translation here than in the previous stories, in order to make the English version more accessible to 21st century readers. There are also a few footnotes, some of which are Karamzin's own, and others added by me where I felt it would be useful.

Given the blatant links to the story of Actaeon (so much so that the final chapter is entitled *The New Actaeon*), I wanted to include Ovid's story for the purposes of comparison. When deliberating over which of the many eloquent and scholarly English translations to use, though, I figured it would be in keeping with Karamzin's tongue-in-cheek tone to abandon these, and 'translate' the story into the dialect of my native Yorkshire. Hopefully, my retelling of the tale, loosely based on Henry Thomas Riley's English translation, will bring the collection to an appropriately light-hearted conclusion.

A Knight of Our Time
by Nikolai Mikhailovich Karamzin

Historical novels came into fashion some time ago. A restless race, known as 'authors', is troubled by sacred relics of the likes of Numa, Aurelius, Alfred and Carloman[14], and profiting from a right (it was hardly *right*) appropriated long ago, these people summon ancient heroes from out of their 'cramped homes' (as Ossian puts it), so that, as they step out onto the stage, they might amuse us with their stories. What a wonderful puppet comedy! One character emerges from the tomb in a long Roman *toga*, with a head of grey hair; another in a short Hispanic mantle, with a black moustache, and each of them rubs his eyes as he commences his tale from the very beginning. However, having grown accustomed to their deep slumbers in the grave, they often yawn... and the readers of these historical fairy tales yawn along with them. I have never been a keen follower of fashion in terms of clothing, I have no desire to follow writing fashions, I do not wish to awaken the sleeping giants of humanity, and I would not like my readers to yawn. So, for that

---

[14] Here, the author is referring to pseudo-historical novels popular at that time, in particular Kheraskov's 'Numa, or Flourishing Rome'. (Translator's note)

reason, instead of a *historical novel*, I plan to tell the *romantic story* of an acquaintance of mine. Meanwhile, *if it is not to your liking, then do not listen*, but *do not prevent me from speaking*: that is my blameless right!

Chapter I
THE BIRTH OF MY HERO

If you ask, 'Who is he?' then I... will not tell you. 'A name is not a person,' they used to say in ancient Russia. However, I will describe so very vividly to you all the qualities of my acquaintance – his facial features, height and bearing – so that you will laugh and point your finger at him, saying, 'So, is he alive after all?' Without a doubt, and if necessary, I can prove that I am not a liar and did not invent a single one of his words or actions; neither the sad ones nor the humorous ones. Nevertheless, I need to give him a name, since too many personal pronouns would be uncomfortable. Therefore, let us call him Leon.

On the meadow-lined side of the Volga, where the clear river Sviyaga flows into it, and where, as we know from the story *Nataliya, the Boyar's Daughter*[15], the wrongfully exiled Boyar Lyuboslavsky lived and died, in a small village, Leon's great-grandfather, grandfather and father were all born. Leon himself

---

[15] Another of Karamzin's sentimental tales. (Translator's note)

was born there, too, at a time when nature, like a lovely coquette, was attending to her toilette, tidying herself up, putting on her best spring dress – it was pale white and blushing pink, with spring flowers – looking at herself in a mirror of clear water, and twisting her curls on the treetops; namely, the month of May. At exactly the same moment when his eyes encountered their first ray of earthly light, the nightingale and the robin suddenly began to sing in the nut trees, while the eagle owl and cuckoo cried out from a birch grove. This was both a good and a bad omen, causing the octogenarian midwife to take Leon in her arms and, with a cheerful smile and a sad sigh, foretell that he would have both happiness and misfortune in life, favourable and inclement conditions, wealth and hardship, friends and enemies, and success in love, while infidelity would take him by the horns. The reader will see that this wise old midwife really did possess the gift of prophecy... But we do not want to reveal ahead of time what happened.

Leon's father was a Russian nobleman by birth, a captain who had retired due to injury, a man of about fifty who was neither rich nor destitute, and – most importantly of all – the kindest person. In terms of character, though, he was not at all like

Tristram Shandy's[16] well-known uncle: he was kind in his own particular way, and of Russian build. When he returned to his homeland after the Turkish and Swedish campaigns, he decided to marry – not early by any means – so he married a twenty-year-old beauty, the daughter of his closest neighbour. Despite her young years, she had a surprising tendency towards melancholy, to such an extent that she could sit for days on end, deep in thought. When she spoke, she did so intelligently, coherently, and with impressive eloquence, and when she glanced at someone, that person would want to linger in her eyes, so welcoming and kind were they! She was a beauty of our time! Rest assured, I do not seek to compare her with you, but in order to explain her grace of spirit, I must reveal a secret that she knew to be cruel. It weighed cruelly on her that the mother of our hero would never have been his father's wife if Cruelty itself had picked the first violet on the banks of the Sviyaga one April! The reader may already have guessed, but if not then wait a little, perhaps. Time removes the veil from dark happenings. Let us merely say that our village beauty was immaculate in body and soul when she married, and that she genuinely loved her husband,

---

[16] *The Life and Opinions of Tristram Shandy, Gentleman*, a novel by Laurence Sterne, published in nine volumes from 1759 to 1767. (Translator's note)

firstly for his kindness, and secondly because there was no-one else for her heart... it was already taken.

Chapter II
HOW HE WAS BORN

Young couples, waiting with tender eagerness for the fruit of your marital union! If you are hoping for a son, how do you imagine him? Handsome? Leon was. White and plump with little rosy cheeks, a little Greek nose, dark little eyes, and coffee-coloured hair on his little round head: is that not so? Leon was like that. Now you have an idea of him, so kiss him in your thoughts, and with an affectionate smile encourage the child to live in the world, and me to be his historian!

Chapter III
HIS FIRST INFANCY

What is there to say about infancy? It is too simple, too innocent, and therefore not a source of curiosity for us, tainted people that we are. I am not disputing the fact that, in a certain sense, it can be called a happy time, the true Arcadia of life, but there is nothing to write about it. Passions, passions! No matter how cruel you may be, or how detrimental to our peace of mind, without you there is nothing delightful in the world. Without you our lives are like insipid water, and a person is a puppet. Without you there are no moving stories, no entertaining novels. We might call infancy a beautiful meadow which is good to look at, and which can be praised in two or three words, but I do not advise any poet to describe it in detail. Terrible, wild rockfaces, roaring rivers, dark forests and African deserts have a more powerful effect than the Vale of Tempe[17] on the imagination. How? Why? I do not know. But I do know that even the most caring friend of children, who constantly praises their innocence and happiness, will soon yawn and doze off if his eyes or thoughts are not presented with something contrary to this innocence and happiness.

However, the reader will offend me if he thinks that I am attempting to cover up the sandy barrenness of my imagination by inserting this comment as a full stop. No, no! I swear by Apollo that I could find enough flowers to adorn this chapter. I could, without deviating from the historical truth, describe the tenderness of Leon's parents in vivid colours. Without violating any of Aristotle's or Horatio's laws, I could move the words around a dozen times, soaring swiftly upwards and plunging smoothly back down again, whether drawing with a pencil or

---

[17] The Vale of Tempe is a gorge in northern Greece. According to legend, it was cut out of the rocks by Poseidon's trident. (Translator's note)

painting with a brush, mixing the mind's important thoughts with the heart's touching emotions. I could say, for example:

'At that time, there was no *Émile* in which Jean-Jacques Rousseau so eloquently, so convincingly talks about the sacred duty of a mother. Upon reading this, the beautiful Emilia, dear Lydia, would henceforth have rejected glittering gatherings and exposed her tender breasts not with the intention of seducing the eyes of young pleasure-seekers, but only for the purpose of feeding her infant. At that time, Rousseau had not yet spoken, but nature had made its voice heard, and our hero's mother nursed him herself. Thus, it was not surprising that, at the dawn of his life, Leon cried, screamed and succumbed to illness less than other babies: the milk of loving mothers is the best nourishment and medicine for children. From the cradle to a small bed, from a tin rattle to a little painted hobbyhorse, from the first babbling sounds to the distinct articulation of words, Leon knew no constraint, coercion, grief or pangs of the heart. He was fed, warmed, comforted and cheered by love: it was the first influence on his soul, and the first colour and mark on the blank page of its sensitivity[18]. External objects had already begun to stir up his attention,

---

[18] Locke states that the soul of a new-born child is a 'blank slate' or 'tabula rasa'.

and with his eyes, hand gestures and words, he would often ask his mother, 'What am I seeing? What am I hearing?'. He had already learned to walk and run, but nothing occupied him so much as his mother's caresses, and no question did he repeat as often as, 'Mama! What do you need?' Never did he want to part from her, and he only learned to walk by following her.'

Is it not true that one such as this could be loved by another? Here is indeed a painting, with antitheses, and a pleasant play on words. But I could go further still; I could add:

'This is the basis of his character! The first part of someone's upbringing almost always decides that person's destiny and principal characteristics. Leon's soul was formed *by* love and *for* love. Now try deceiving him and tormenting him, cruel people! He will sigh and weep, but never – or at least not for a very long time – will his heart be weaned away from the sweet inclination to delight in the heart of another; never will he turn away from the gentle habit of living for someone else, in spite of any sadness, or the raging storms that stir up the lives of the sensitive. In the same way, a faithful sunflower will never cease to turn towards the sun. It will keep its face turned to the luminary of the daytime even when storm clouds obscure it, whether it be morning or evening, and even when it begins to wither and dry out: it goes on following the sun until the last moment of its existence as a plant!'

I hope that Zoilus[19] alone would fail to praise this passage, especially the new, striking comparison between sensitive hearts, ever striving towards love, and the sunflower which always tilts itself towards the sun. I hope that some of my dear readers might sigh from the depths of their hearts and order this flower to be engraved on their seals.

'The end of the chapter!' the reader will say. But no. There is still much more that I could think up and describe. I could fill ten, or even twenty pages with a description of Leon's childhood; for example how his mother was his only dictionary – that is, how she taught him to speak and how he, forgetting other words, heeded and remembered every one of hers; how he, while already knowing the names of all the birds which fluttered around their garden and in the woods, and all the flowers that grew in the meadows and fields, still did not know the names of the wicked people of the world nor anything of their deeds; how his soul developed its first abilities; how it quickly took in the actions of the things around him, such as the springtime meadow greedily drinking the first of the spring rain; how thoughts and feelings emerged in his soul, like the fresh April

---

[19] A Greek philosopher, known for his criticism of Homer. (Translator's note)

greenery; how so many times every day and every minute his tender mother kissed him, wept, and gave thanks to heaven; how so many times he put his tiny arms around her, pressing himself against her breast; how his voice said, more and more firmly, 'I love you, Mama!', and how from time to time his heart felt this more vividly than ever!

My words would flow like a river, if only I were inclined to go into detail, but I do not want to. I do not want to! There is still much that I must describe, but I will save paper and the reader's patience, and... thus this is the end of the chapter!

Chapter IV,
WHICH IS WRITTEN ONLY FOR THE SAKE OF CHAPTER FIVE

Ladies and gentlemen! You are not reading a novel, but a true story: consequently, the author is under no obligation to account for what took place. *It actually happened that way!* So, I will not say another word on the matter. Is that apt? Is it really relevant? That is not my business. I simply follow Fate, pen in hand, and describe what it does in its omnipotence. But why? Ask Fate itself; though I must tell you in advance that you will receive no reply. For seven thousand years (if the chroniclers are to be believed), it has been performing miracles in the world and has never explained them to anyone. If we take a glance at history, or look at what is going on around us, the riddles of the Sphinx are everywhere, and not even Oedipus can solve them. The rose may wither, but the thorns remain; and a hundred-year-old oak, succour of travellers, may be struck down by lightening, while a poisonous tree stands unharmed all the way to its roots. Peter the Great turned cold in the embrace of death whilst busying himself with plans for the good of the country; meanwhile it is not uncommon for a worthless person to enter a second century. A fortunate young fellow, whose life has been smiled upon by destiny and by nature, so to speak, can be extinguished in a moment, like a meteor, while some hapless, superfluous wretch who is a burden to himself, lives and cannot wait for his end to come... What can we do? Weep, those who have tears, but from time to time take comfort in the thought that this world is only the prologue to the play!

Chapter V
FATE'S FIRST BLOW

The north wind blew over the gentle mother's delicate breast, and the genius of her life extinguished its torch! Yes, dear reader, she caught a cold, and on the ninth day she was moved from a soft bed to a hard one – a coffin – and from there into the ground. Then everyone dispersed, as is customary, and the world forgot, as is customary... But no; let us talk a little more about her final moments.

Our hero was seven years old at the time. During his mother's illness, he would not leave her bedside. He sat or stood next to her, gazed constantly into her eyes, and asked, 'Do you feel better, Mama?'

'Yes, I feel better,' she said, when she was able to speak. She looked at him, and her eyes filled with tears, so she stared up at the heavens. She wanted to caress her heart's beloved, but was afraid to pass her illness on to him, so sometimes she would say with a smile, 'Sit beside me,' and at other times she would sigh and tell him, 'Go away from me!' Ah! He would only heed the first of these; he refused to obey the other.

He had to be forcibly dragged away from the dying woman. 'Wait, wait!' he cried through his tears. 'Mama wants to tell me something; I won't go. No, I won't!' But in the meantime, his mother left this world.

When they carried him out, people tried in vain to comfort him. He kept repeating one phrase: 'I want to go to my dear Mama!' Eventually he escaped from the arms of his nurse and ran off to see his mother lying dead on the table. He clutched her hand – it was like wood – and pressed his face against hers – it was like ice... 'Ah, dearest Mama!' he cried, and fell to the ground. He was carried out again, now sick with a high fever.

The father was devastated and wept, for he loved his wife as much as it is possible to love. His heart had already known grief in his life, but this fatal blow seemed to be the ultimate misfortune...

Pale-faced, and his grey hair dishevelled, the father stood beside the coffin as the prayers were sung for the deceased. Sobbing, he bade farewell to her, kissing her face and hands with fervour, then bent down towards the grave, where he threw the first handful of earth onto the coffin. On his knees, he raised his eyes and arms and said, 'Your soul is in heaven! I do not have long left to live!' then walked home, treading softly. His son was lying unconscious, so he sat at his bedside and thought, 'Are you really going to follow your mother? Are you really going to leave me all alone? May it be done according to the Lord's will!'

Leon opened his eyes, rose, and held his hand out to his father, saying: 'Where is she? Where is she?'

'With the angels, my friend!'

'Will she not come back to us?'

'We will go to her.'

'Soon?'

'Soon, my friend. Time passes quickly, even for those who mourn.'

They embraced and wept, the old man and the child shedding tears together! Then they began to feel better.

Oh, salutary time, hasten to pour out your healing balm onto their wounded hearts! May you, like Morpheus, scatter the poppies of oblivion: sprinkle some of those flowers over my young hero. Ah, he is not yet old enough for such profound, never-ending anguish: there will be many, many more opportunities for him to grieve in his life! Spare his childhood! And do not forget to comfort the old man, too: he has always been a kind person. His hands, armed in the harsh duty of war, killed proud enemies, but his heart never participated in the killing, and never did his feet, in the heat of battle, trample inhumanely over the bodies of unfortunate victims: he loved to bury them and pray for the salvation of their souls. Salutary time, comfort the old man, and give him a few more peaceful years, if only so that he can devote them to raising his son. May they sometimes recall their loved one, but without anguish and suffering, and may the pain of grief occasionally resonate in their hearts, but ever quieter, like an echo that comes back weaker every time, until at last... it is silent.

My dear reader! I want the thought of the deceased to remain in your heart: may she be hidden in its depths, but never disappear! One day we will hand you a small notebook, and the thought will be awakened: then tears will glisten in your eyes. Otherwise... I am no author.

Chapter VI
ACADEMIC SUCCESS, THE EDUCATED MIND, AND FEELINGS

Thus, fleeting time wiped away the tears of grief with its wings, and everyone went back to their work; the father to the farm, and the son to his textbooks. The local deacon, the most renowned scholar in the district, was Leon's first teacher and could not praise his intellect highly enough. 'Three days,' he said, describing the miracle to other scholars. 'It took him three days to learn all the letters, and a week for all the combinations; then one more and he could make out words and titles. Such a thing has never been seen or heard of before! This child will go far.'

He did indeed have an unusual capacity for understanding, and after a few months he could read all the church books, such as *Our Father*. He learned to write just as quickly, as well as beginning to fathom the secular press, to the astonishment of the neighbouring gentry to whom Leon's father often made him read so that his heart might rejoice in their praise. The first secular book which our little hero learned by heart after reading it over and over, was Aesop's *Fables*; hence why, throughout his life, he had an unusual respect for creatures who could not talk, recalling their wise judgements in the Greek sage's book, and often, upon seeing the foolishness of people, he regretted that they did not have the sense of Aesop's beasts.

Soon, Leon was given the key to the yellow cabinet in which his deceased mother's library was kept, and where there were two shelves of novels and a third with a few spiritual books: this was an important stage in the education of his mind and heart! *Daïra, histoire orientale, Selim and Damasina, Miramond,* and *The Story of Lord N.* were all read in a single summer, with such curiosity and such real pleasure that a different parent might have found frightening, but Leon's father could not help being pleased, supposing that this eagerness to read any kind of book was a good sign in a child. Occasionally, though, in the evenings, he would tell his son, 'Leon, do not strain your eyes! It will be light again tomorrow and you will have more time for reading.' To himself, however, he thought, 'He takes after his mother! She was never without a book in her hands. Darling child, be like her in all things, but live longer!'

But what was it about the novels that captivated him? Did the portrayal of love really hold so much charm for an eight- to ten-year-old boy, making him forget about the fun games for children of his age and spend days on end sitting in one place, all of his childish attention absorbed, as it were, in the shenanigans of *Miramond* or *Daïra*? No, Leon was more concerned with happenings, and with the connection between things and events, rather than the emotions of romantic love. Nature throws us into the world, as if into a dark, dense forest, with no ideas or information, but with a huge supply of curiosity which begins to take effect during early childhood: the earlier it does, the more tender and perfect the soul's natural foundation will be. This is the white cloud at the dawn of life, from behind which the light of knowledge and experience soon appears! If it were to be placed on weighing scales, with those thoughts and information accumulated within the soul over the course of ten weeks of childhood on one side, and the ideas and knowledge acquired by an adult mind over a period of ten years on the other, then there is no doubt that the scales would tip under the weight of the former. Kind nature is in a hurry to bestow upon a new-born child everything he needs for his earthly journey: his mind soars like an eagle at the start of life's expanse, but where the object of our curiosity is merely speculation instead of a genuine need, then the soaring turns into walking and the steps become more difficult with every passing hour.

Through novels, a new world revealed itself to Leon. As if in a magic lantern, he saw a multitude of different people on a stage, and a multitude of wondrous deeds and adventures: the workings of Fate which had hitherto been unknown to him... (Nevertheless, a heartfelt premonition told him, 'Ah! You, too, will fall victim to it one day! The whirlwind will catch hold of you and whisk you away... To where? To where?'). New canvasses constantly rose up before his eyes: landscape after landscape, and group after group appeared to him. Leon's soul sailed through the world of books, like Christopher Columbus on the Atlantic Ocean, on a voyage ... a quest to find the undiscovered.

Not only did this reading fail to harm his young soul, but it was also rather helpful for the formation of his moral sensibility. In *Daïra*, *Miramond* and *Selim and Damasina* (does the reader know these?), in fact in all the novels from the yellow cabinet, the heroes and heroines remained virtuous, despite the many temptations of fate, and all the villains were described in the blackest shades. The former triumphed in the end, while the latter ultimately vanished, like dust. Inconspicuously, but indelibly, Leon's heart drew a conclusion: 'Thus, decency and virtue are one and the same! Therefore, evil is hideous and repulsive! Hence, the virtuous person always wins, while the wicked person perishes!' Such sensibility is life-saving, as it provides a firm support for good morals, and does not need to be proven. Ah! Leon would often see something objectionable in perfect summers, yet his heart would not stray from its comforting system: despite the obvious, he would say, 'No, no! The triumph of vice is a trick and an illusion!'

> *No, no! By this brilliance I will not*
> *be blinded, no matter what!*
> *The dragon is lulled to sleep for a while,*
> *but his very dream itself is vile!*
> *A villain builds a house on Mount Etna*
> *and beneath his feet is ash and cinders*
> *(there the lava with flowers is strewn,*
> *and thunder in the silence looms).*
> *May he know no remorse all his days!*
> *He does not deserve to know its ways:*
> *insensitivity is as hell to one,*
> *who, without regret, evil deeds has done!*

It was with such lively delight that, at six or seven o'clock on a summer's morning, our little hero would kiss his father's hand, and hurry with a book to the high banks of the Volga, among the nut trees, and beneath the shade of an ancient oak! There, in his white jacket, throwing himself onto the ground among the wildflowers, he looked like the most beautiful, animate flower. His light brown hair, as soft as silk, fluttered in the breeze, around his dear little rosy face. His cap served as a little table, and he would put his book on it, one hand supporting his head, and the other turning the pages, in time with his big blue eyes as they flew from one page to the next, and which, like a clear mirror, reflected all the passions, whether good or bad, described in the novel: surprise, joy, fear, regret or grief. Sometimes, setting the book aside, he would gaze at the blue expanse of the Volga, the white sails of the ships and boats, and the flocks of fishers as they boldly descended from beneath the clouds and into the foaming waves, only to soar back up into the air a moment later. This scene made such an impression on his young soul that, twenty years later, at the height of his passions, his burning heart at its busiest, he could not see a large river with sailing vessels and flying fishers without a certain joyous stirring: it brought to mind the Volga, his homeland, and his carefree youth, touching his soul, and causing him to shed a tear. Anyone who has not experienced the gentle power of similar memories has not known the sweetest sensation. Home, the April of life, and the first flowers of the soul's spring! How dear you are to anyone born with a gracious inclination towards melancholy!

Chapter VII
PROVIDENCE

That summer, Leon's heart had a vivid sense of the Almighty, and he would be unable to remember it without emotion for the rest of his life. The notion of divinity was one of his first thoughts. His dear mother had tried her very best to instil this in Leon's heart. When picking a spring flower from the meadow, or summer fruits for him from the garden, she would always say, 'God gives us flowers, and God gives us fruits!'

'God!' the curious boy once repeated. 'Who is he, Mama?'

'The heavenly father of all people, who feeds them and does everything good for them. He gave you to me, and me to you.'

'You, dear Mama? He really is kind! I will always love him!'

'Love him and pray to him every day.'

'How should I pray?'

'Say, 'Lord, have mercy on us!''

'I will, I will, dear Mama!'

From that day onward, Leon always prayed to God. Ah! He prayed to him with tears in his eyes during his mother's illness! But higher destinies are unfathomable. Such was Leon's religion from that summer until the event which I now wish to describe.

One hot day, he was reading a book as usual in the shade of the ancient oak, his elderly uncle sitting on the grass some ten paces away from him. Suddenly a cloud appeared, and the sun was covered with a dark haze. Leon's uncle called to him to go home. 'Wait a moment,' he replied, without looking up from his book. Lightning flashed, thunder rumbled, and the rain came down. The old man really wanted to go home. Leon wrapped the book in a shawl, stood up, and looked at the stormy sky. The storm was intensifying, yet he admired a flash of lightning and walked softly, without the slightest fear. Suddenly, a bear came running out of the forest, and headed straight for Leon. The uncle dared not even cry out in terror. Twenty paces separated our little friend from inevitable death, but he was lost in thought and could not see the danger. One more second, maybe two, and the poor boy would fall victim to this ferocious beast. There was a terrible clap of thunder... such as Leon had never heard before. It seemed as if the sky above him was being torn apart and the lightning was wrapping itself around his head. He closed his eyes, fell to his knees, and all he could say was, 'Dear God!' Half a minute later, he opened his eyes and saw the bear in front of him, struck dead by the lightning. His uncle managed to pull himself together, and he told the boy by what miracle God had saved him. Still kneeling, Leon was shaking with fear and from the effects of the electrical force. Eventually, he raised his eyes heavenwards, and heedless of the thick, black clouds, he could see and sense the presence of God – his Saviour. His tears poured down like hail; he prayed in the very depths of his soul, with an ardent fervour unusual for a child; and his prayer was... one of thanksgiving! Leon would never be an atheist after that, even if he did read Spinoza, Hobbes, and *The System of Nature*.

Dear reader! Believe it or not, this event is not a figment of the imagination. I could have changed the bear to the noblest lion or tiger... if such animals existed in Russia.

Chapter VIII
THE FRATERNITY OF PROVINCIAL NOBLEMEN

I know that everything happens for the best: I am aware of the advantages of our time, and I rejoice in the successes of enlightenment in Russia. However, it also gives me pleasure to turn my gaze to those times when our gentry, having retired, returned to their homeland in order that they may never again be parted from their peaceful hearth and home. They rarely so much as glanced at the city, living out their days in freedom, without a care. It is true that they sometimes found the isolation tedious, but they also knew how to enjoy themselves when they came together. Am I mistaken? Nevertheless, it seems to me that they possessed plenty of character, too; something special which we no longer find in the provinces, and which, if nothing else, entertains the imagination. Enlightenment brings the abilities of nations and people closer together, levelling them out, like trees in a tended garden.

Captain Radushin, Leon's father, loved to entertain the kind acquaintances whom God sent his way. Each time, his son would run to him with great enthusiasm, and tell him, 'Father! Guests are coming!', to which our captain would reply, 'They are most welcome!' Then he would put on his rounded wig and go out to meet them with a joyful expression. The way to be bored by people is to be with them constantly, and the way to really enjoy their company is to see them only occasionally. Our provincial folk never tired of talking with each other: they were not familiar with the beasts of politics and literature, yet they discussed, debated, and made a lot of noise. Rural farming, hunting, well-known lawsuits from around the province, and anecdotes from bygone times provided a wealth of material for tales and commentary... Ah! Death and time have long since cast a dark shroud of oblivion over you, knights of the S. district, faithful friends of Captain

Radushin! Neither Le Brun[20] nor Lampi[21] preserved your image for us. However, I am not writing Leon's story for nothing: the mirror of my memory is clear. I am looking at you now, honourable Major Thaddeus Gromilov, in your large black wig, wearing your crimson velvet jerkin in winter and summer alike, with a dagger on your hip, and yellow Tatar boots. I can hear how you, unaccustomed as you are to walking on tiptoes in the salons of noble gentlemen, stamp your feet from two rooms away and make yourself known from a distance with your loud voice which a company of land-militia once obeyed and whose clear tones would frequently strike terror among the bad military leaders of the province! I can see you, too, grey-haired Cavalry Master Burilov, shot by a Bashkir arrow on the steppes of Ufa; your legs are weak, but your soul is steadfast; you walk with a cane, but wave it about vigorously when you need to vividly describe either your squadron's offensive or your disgust at the dishonest deed of some unworthy nobleman in your district! I glance at your important stance, former Commander Pryamodushin, as well as at your aquiline nose, by which the provincial secretary cannot pull you along, since conscience is cleverer

---

[20] Élisabeth Louise Vigée Le Brun (1755-1842), French portrait painter. (Translator's note)
[21] Johann Baptist von Lampi (1751-1830), Austrian-Italian portrait painter. (Translator's note)

than chicanery. I see how, when you talk about Biron and the Secret Chancellery, you lean on your long cane with its silver pommel, which was given to you by Field Marshal Minikh... I can see you all, worthy provincial matadors whose conversation influenced the character of my hero, and in order to vividly portray the nobility of your hearts to the full, I shall list here the conditions agreed among yourselves in the home of Leon's father and recorded in Pryamodushin's hand...

FRATERNITY AGREEMENT

'We, the undersigned, swear, by our honour as noble people, to live and die as brothers, to stand steadfast behind each other in all circumstances, to spare neither effort nor money in mutual service, to always act with unanimity, to observe the common good of the nobility, to stand up for the oppressed, to heed the Russian saying, 'a nobleman is one behind many others', to fear neither the grand nor the powerful, but only God and Sovereign, to boldly speak the truth to governors and military leaders, to never be their hangers-on, and never to act against our conscience. If any of us should fail to uphold this oath, he will be shamed and expelled from the fraternity.'

Eight names follow.

Although a secret chronicle tells me that this friendly society of our noblemen was concluded on the day of Leon's birth, which his father always celebrated with great fervour and notable opulence (so much so that he even sent to the city for fresh lemons), and although the reader will guess that on such a happy day, especially towards evening, the host and his guests may not have been in their usual state of mind and heart; since...

Knee-deep in the delights of Bacchus we stand,
Thus, are we all mighty heroes with glass in hand;

history, nevertheless, which lies year in year out (on 1st April and 29th February), made sure that, when they awoke the next day, they re-read their declaration, confirmed it all over again, and (even though the great European powers do not always do this) endeavoured to carry it out to the letter. Death alone could destroy their fraternal bond... At this point I would like to look ahead. There is still a long time to wait; but then, perhaps, amidst the wealth of events, I might forget this admirable quality. Therefore, I will say this... When fate had played with Leon for a while in the big wide world, it threw him back into his homeland, where he found Major Gromilov sitting over the infirm Pryamodushin who was lying paralysed, having lost the use of his arms (all their other friends were already in the next world). Gromilov was feeding the patient with his own hands and weeping bitterly as he said to Leon, 'It is a sickening thing to be orphaned in old age!' Such kind people! May you rest in peace! Others may call you savages, but as a child, Leon listened with pleasure to your verbose conversations, and it was from you that he borrowed his Russian amiability and the spirit of Russian and noble pride, which he later could not find even among the boyars, since it cannot be replaced by arrogance and haughtiness, noble pride being a sense of one's own worthiness, distancing a person from vice and despicable acts. Kind old gentlemen! May you rest in peace!

Chapter IX
REVERIE AND A MELANCHOLIC DISPOSITION

So, Leon read books, ran to meet visitors from time to time, sometimes went himself to visit kind provincial nobles, listened to their stories, and so on. There was plenty to keep him busy, but he still had time to think and dream. Despite my little weakness for novels, I must admit that they can be a hothouse for a young soul who might mature ahead of time after reading them; and this, if philosophising doctors are to be believed, can be dangerous… for the health, at least. 'You are ruining yourself with books and novels!' exclaimed one eminent doctor. 'Do not meddle with nature's unfinished work; do not inflame children's imaginations; allow young nerves to strengthen, and avoid straining them if you do not want life's balance to be upset from the very beginning!' By his tenth year, Leon could already spend a couple of hours imagining and building castles in the air. Perils and heroic friendships were the favourite subject of his musings. It must be noted that he always imagined himself as the one who saved people from these perils, and not the bringer of danger: this was a sign of a proud, glorious heart! In his thoughts, our hero might fly through the darkness of the night, responding to the call of a traveller who was being attacked by robbers, or he would take a high tower by storm, where his friend was suffering and in chains. This kind of Don Quixote-style imagination was an indicator of the moral path that Leon's life would take. Doubtless, you phlegmatic people who do not live but doze in the world and weep from just a single yawn, will not have experienced such dreams in your own childhood! And you, too, prudent egoists who do not become attached to people, instead merely remaining carefully behind them until your connection with them becomes useful, then freely withdrawing your hand as soon as they might be about to demand something of you! My hero would take off his little cap, bow down low to you, and say respectfully, 'My dear sirs, you will never see me flying your flag!'

In addition, he loved to feel sad without knowing why. Poor thing! Could an early tendency towards melancholy be an indication of woes to come? Leon's eyes shone through a kind of veil, a transparent curtain of sensibility. The sad loss of his mother heightened this natural melancholic disposition still further. Ah! Even the very best father cannot replace a mother, the gentlest creature on earth! Only a woman's love, always attentive and caring, can satisfy the heart in all relationships! Thus nature, destiny and novels prepared Leon for what was to happen next.

Chapter X
AN IMPORTANT ACQUAINTANCE

Count Mirov, a resident of the capital and a wealthy man who had once served with Captain Radushin and wanted to revive their old friendship, came to live in his neighbourhood... The captain went with his son to visit him. It was the first time Leon had seen a large house, a multitude of servants, opulence, and lavishly decorated rooms, and he walked behind his father with a timid expression on his face. It was no wonder that he bowed awkwardly to their host, kept shifting from one foot to the other, and knew neither which way to look nor what to do with his hands. The count's stern expression (he was a man of about fifty years of age) served to increase his shyness all the more. However, when he glanced at the kindly-looking countess, Leon felt happier... He glanced at her again, and suddenly his face changed. He burst into tears, and tried in vain to hide it. This surprised the hosts; they wanted to know the cause of his tears, and asked him questions, but he said nothing. His father ordered him to speak, so Leon replied quietly, 'The countess looks like my mother.'

The captain looked for himself and said, 'It is true. Please forgive us, madame.' Then he, too, began to shed tears of grief. Leon forgot everything and flung his arms around him... The count was cold, but the countess, who not altogether coincidentally happened to resemble Leon's mother, wiped her eyes with a handkerchief. Her usually pale face was flushed with fresh colour... Oh, women! What stirrings of sensibility cannot be found at the heart of your faithful responses? Leon looked at Emilia (that was the name of the countess) with a touching, genuine gratitude, and Emilia looked at Leon with tender affection. Everything that separated the twenty-five-year-old lady of high society from the nine-year-old village boy vanished in a minute of empathy... but that minute turned into hours, days and months. I must now tell you something strange... It was easy to love our hero, who was fair of face, good-looking, sensitive and intelligent, but to become ardently attached to this innocent child, with all the signs of real passion, that is what I would call an inexplicable oddity! Have women ever really been explicable, though? Meanwhile, I must introduce the reader to the countess.

Chapter XI
AN EXTRACT FROM THE STORY OF THE COUNTESS

'L'histoire d'une femme est toujours un roman,' (A woman's story is always a novel), a Frenchman once said, meaning that which is known to everyone. Love, of course, is an important part of their lives: men can be unhappy without it, too, of course, but they can forget themselves and engage in self-deception, seeing the means as the end, while beautiful women constantly strive towards a single goal, and the saying 'to live is to love' is for them a mathematical truth. No-one will be surprised if I say that, to the countess, the count was just a husband, that is, a person who was sometimes bearable, sometimes necessary, and sometimes extremely dull. However, if I mention that, before she came to the village, the countess, being delightful and kind, was able to maintain a quietness of heart, and not by chance (since chance is often the guardian of a man's innocence), but systematically and with common sense, which might cause the most credulous reader to smile... So much the worse for the morals of our time! When my hero entered society, he asked about the countess, and everyone spoke of her with respect. Fifty-year-old spinsters would assure him that Moscow's gossip papers only mentioned her on rare occasions, and then only in passing, attributing some kind of fleeting coquetry to her, or (this is a technical term, unknown to the laity!) a sprinkling of flirtatiousness, which disappeared with the first stirring of reason and was never of any consequence. I cannot speak for any one else, but after this testimony I am inclined to believe the contents of the following letter from the countess, written on the day she left, and addressed to a faithful friend who later gave it to Leon. In the absence of other biographical materials, it will serve as an outline of the countess's story:

Forgive me, my dear! We have been travelling for two hours. For God's sake, do not scold my husband who took it into his head to concern himself with economy in January! I swear to you that I will not miss Moscow, as I am not leaving anything pleasant behind, and I have been bored there ever since you moved away. You do not believe my indifference towards worldly pleasures, saying, 'Let ugly women hate the mirror; beauty and grace will eagerly look into it, and society is our mirror!' Nevertheless, it is true that I have no desire to deceive you. As soon as a woman has no desire to be a coquette, then glittering banquets and balls no longer captivate her. Despite men's slander, we do sometimes reason, and we have rules which we follow. Everything that I have seen in society has convinced me all the more of the need to restrain the stirrings of our flighty hearts and our self-love. I believe that fiery passions do have heavenly moments; but they are only moments! I would like to live in heaven, though: if I cannot, then I would prefer not to know it. A married woman must either find happiness at home, or magnanimously renounce it: fate did not grant me the former, so I must take comfort in magnanimity. Is it not true that we rarely see either of these? Consequently, I have something to boast about in life. Not being Rousseau's Julia, thank goodness, I would prefer the gentle Saint Preux to the judicious Wolmar, but despite the difference in years, I would be able to respect my husband, even if he was Wolmar! My count, though, is utterly stoic; he will not become attached to anything perishable, and is not ashamed to say why he married me! A husband like that, who has left his heart with nothing to do, keeps his mind and his rules very busy indeed. For my first two years with him, I was unhappy; I tried, to no avail, every means of drawing him out of his deadly indifference – even jealousy itself – but I eventually calmed down. If providence grants my heart's one wish – to be a mother – then I will leave to my children the legacy of my unsullied name. I have earned happiness at least, and nothing could prevent me from taking pleasure in it; I have feared neither the probing eyes of slander, nor the opinions of strict people!

That said, before our departure I almost found myself in a dangerous situation! Just imagine, the languid N. who had visited our house six or seven times, took it upon himself to write me a love letter! The poor young man! He was so adept at speaking to a woman's heart: he flattered my self-esteem so well, without uttering a word, but simply looking at me and at other women! He may have cast immodest glances from time to time, but that bold letter required decisive measures: he was banned from the house![22] *In my usual way, I brought the count a new declaration of love, appropriately written on pink paper*[23]. *As was his wont, he did not read it, but secreted it in his bureau, giving me his word that when he was in the countryside, he would read all the letters from my unfortunate Célandons in moments of boredom. It was a clever ruse! The count can sometimes be amusing and has recently been almost affectionate. It could be said that he and I have lived together as soulmates from the moment when I stopped looking for his soul! He wanted to take an Italian singer and another two or three musicians with us to the country, for my entertainment, but I refused: music*

---

[22] It is important to remember that this was in ancient times, or at least a very long time ago.

[23] Bygone days again! People no longer write on pink paper in such situations.

makes me sad, and its effects might be even more powerful in isolation... I am even thinking of giving up novels: why excite the heart and imagination with thoughts when my well-being should come from calmness?

I could not decipher the last ten lines at all: they had become almost completely worn away over time: this is a frequent problem to those of us who deal with antique objects! However, by now the readers already have a vague idea about Emilia's character, intellect and principles. Something must now be said about her appearance, as this is far from unimportant to women. They themselves are quite certain about that, and a good-natured woman will forgive constant insults, unless those careless words concern her beauty... Were I to see a lovely portrait of the countess and say, 'But painters are such flatterers!' for example. I have further evidence. To this day, my hero still speaks with rapture about the countess's blue, angelic eyes, her gentle smile, her slender, Diana-like figure, and her long, chestnut-brown hair... Once again, readers might interrupt me by pointing out that describing romantic heads is just the same as the painter's flattering... That may be true, but I will dispel doubt by declaring at last that Count Mirov himself, with whom I became acquainted in his very old age, would always say when complimenting a beautiful woman, 'She is almost as beautiful as my countess was in her youth.'

The husband's testimony concerning his wife's beauty would be accepted in any court: so, in addition to her blue eyes, gentle smile, slender figure and long, chestnut-brown hair, readers may imagine a full complement of everything that we find captivating in women, and think to themselves, 'Countess Mirova was like that!' When it comes to their tastes, I have power of attorney.

Chapter XII
A SECOND MAMA

We have already mentioned Emilia's inexplicable affection for Leon, but let us note a few historical circumstances which help to explain this phenomenon. The honourable Major Thaddeus Gromilov, who knew people as well as he knew *The Articles of War*, and the military leader Pryamodushin[24], whose long, aquiline nose was an undeniable sign of his observant nature, often told Captain Radushin, 'Your son was born under a lucky star: you only have to look at him to love him!' Incidentally, this demonstrates that our old gentlemen, despite not knowing Lavater[25], already possessed an understanding of physiognomy and considered it a gift to be liked by people for one's

---
[24] These have already been mentioned in previous chapters.
[25] Johann Kaspar Lavater, 1741-1801, Swiss physiognomist. (Translator's note)

great prosperity (woe betide anyone who is unable to appreciate it!)... Leon slipped easily into love, with a kind of welcoming expression, a kind of endearing gaze, and a kind of soft lilt to his voice that echoed pleasantly in hearts. The countess had seen him during an exquisite moment of sensitivity – weeping over a fond memory that she had herself evoked. So much good came out of that for our hero! It must also be said that, despite Emilia's wise principles and her great prudence, she was beginning to suffer from boredom in the country, where she spent her days face to face with her staid husband. How nice it was to lavish affection upon this dear little boy! He had grown up shy and awkward in the country. How lovely to take him by the hand! 'Poor little motherless boy! He loved his mother so much! She looked like me! I will prepare this village boy to become an admirable man of society, and what will be a pleasure for me will become a blessing for him!' These must have been the countess's thoughts as she attempted to win Leon over with her affection. Meanwhile, Leon, who could hardly believe his luck, accepted her attentiveness with sensitivity, so that, the next time they met, Emilia told him through her tears, 'Leon, I want to take the place of your mama! Will you love me as you loved her?' He rushed over to kiss her hand and began to weep with joy. It seemed to him that his dear mama had come back to life!

So, Emilia declared Leon to be her dear friend; the next day, and eventually every day, she sent a carriage for him; she taught him French herself, and even history and geography, since Leon (let it be said, but we must keep it to ourselves!) as yet had no knowledge of anything apart from Aesop's *Fables*, *Daïra* and the great works of Fyodor Emin. The countess also tried to cultivate his outward appearance, too, showing him how he must walk, bow, and move with ease, but our hero had no need of a dance master. Of course, she dressed him in the latest fashion: that was a small weakness on the part of women! Loving to dress up themselves, they also loved to dress up those who had the good fortune to be liked by them. After two weeks, the neighbours did not recognise Leon in his stylish frock coat and English cap, with Emilia's cane in his hands and a perfect, city-style walk. 'What a miracle!' they said, although the miracle could be explained away by the fact that a lady of high society was busy working on our little country boy.

His father said to him, 'Leon! You and I hardly ever see each other, but I am pleased that you are loved by good hearts. Because of the countess's kindness, you will become somebody!' His achievements in French were more amazing still: without ever setting eyes on a dull grammar book, after three months he could already express his grateful love to his mama, and he knew absolutely all the subtleties of affectionate expressions. She was proud of her pupil, and she loved him even more!

Lucky child! If you were eight years older, who would not have envied your good fortune? But you owe your success to your youth itself! Emilia, whom we know for her strict principles, could only love innocence. Who would be afraid of a child, even one who is clever, ardent, and an avid reader of novels? Men in women's dresses can be strange, but innocence has no gender! The countess, meanwhile, warmed Leon with her tender kisses, and without any pang of conscience, when he arrived, cold, and ran into her study: as long as the count was not with her. She never took breakfast without her pupil, no matter how early she rose, just as young wives of elderly husbands are eager to do as the doctor has prescribed. Emilia brewed the coffee herself and he, standing behind her, would comb her light brown hair which almost reached down to the ground, and which he loved to kiss... Such childishness! She allowed him to do other things of that sort. For example, he enjoyed assisting her at her dressing table, so that her maid eventually became so accustomed to his help that she no longer entered her mistress's room when Leon was there... I blush for my hero, but I must admit that he even brought the countess her shoes! 'Could a noble person really stoop so low!' the provincial gentry would say.

Nevertheless, he saw the most beautiful feet in the world!

For him, every minute of learning was a minute of pleasure: picking up a French book, Leon would sit beside his mama – so close that he could feel the beating of her heart – and she would put her head on his shoulder to follow the words on the page after him. Having read a few lines without error, Leon would glance at her and smile, and at that moment their lips would involuntarily meet: success demanded rewards, and he received them! Before lunch, the countess would sit at her harpsichord: she played and sang, and her dear pupil was captivated by the novelty of this heavenly pleasure, his eyes filling with tears, his heart a-flutter, and his soul roused to such an extent that sometimes he would grab Emilia by the hand and say, 'Enough! Enough, Mama!' A moment later, though, he would want to listen again...

The beginning of spring was so wonderful for Leon! The countess loved to go for walks: he was her guide, and with indescribable delight he would show her the lovely places that were home to him. They would often sit on the high banks of the Volga, and with the sound of the waves in the background, Leon would fall asleep on his dear mother's lap. She would be afraid to touch him in case she woke him: the sleep of beauty and innocence seemed so sweet and adorable to her! Watch and enjoy, lovely Emilia! The dawn of sensitivity is quiet and beautiful, but storms are not far away. The heart of your beloved one is maturing together with his mind, and the flower of innocence is subject to the same fate as other flowers! The reader will think that, with this rhetorical flourish, we are preparing him for something that is quite the opposite of innocence. No! There is still time ahead! Only eleven years have passed since our hero was born... Nevertheless, our love for the truth obliges us to describe a small incident which could be interpreted one way or another...

Chapter XIII
THE NEW ACTAEON

Leon knew that, every morning, the countess went to bathe in the little river near her house. One day, having woken early, he dressed hurriedly and, without waiting for the countess's carriage, walked to that very spot in response to some vague but alluring notion. An hour later, he was standing on the riverbank. He could see the path leading from the countess's house, and a patch of trampled grass... 'This must be where the countess undresses, so she will probably come here in a few minutes. I must be quick!' Hiding his clothes in the bushes, he rushed over to the water. The stream was shaded on both sides by tall willow trees. It flowed over clean yellow sand, and having found its way through the shade of the trees, a ray of sunlight seemed to be playing on the riverbed down below. Our hero had never enjoyed bathing so much before, and thought, 'What a lovely place Mama has chosen!' Was it any wonder that he tried to imagine her reflected in the mirror of the water? But he could not! This village boy had never seen a marble statue of Venus, or paintings of Diana bathing! On hot days, he had, it is true, happened to glance at the edge of the pond where the local girls, with their tanned skin... But how could he compare them? It was ridiculous to even think about it! Leon would doubtless have turned to the god of the river, if he had been familiar with mythology, but in his ignorance he assumed that only humble, silent fish dwelt in water!

Suddenly, through the trees in the distance, a white dress came into view... Leon had no time to get dressed: he leapt out of the river and onto the opposite bank, where he lay on the ground among the raspberry bushes... Emilia arrived with her maids, glanced around, then began to undress. What did our little one do? Quietly, he parted the branches of the bush and watched. This would be his undoing! Still, his heart was beating normally, which proved his innocence! Youth is so curious! A child's gaze is so pure and sinless! Nevertheless, it is easiest of all to sin with the eyes: who is afraid of them? After all, misers are allowed to look at their gold! Emilia took off her white blouse and pulled at the muslin shawl that covered her breasts... If the reader is expecting me to paint a picture in the style of the golden age, he is mistaken! Years teach modesty: let the young authors alone break the news to the public that women have arms and legs! We old men know everything: we know everything that can be seen, but we must remain silent. On the other hand, is it necessary to describe, even in a novel, those things which are now there for all to see (thanks to fashion), in gatherings, at balls, and at festivals? Novels describe the phoenix and the firebird, but not the sparrows and swallows which everyone knows. I must look at things solely through the eyes of my hero, and he saw nothing!

Three English hounds ran up behind the countess and leaped into the river. Swimming to the opposite bank, they smelled poor Leon in the grass and began to bark. He took fright and ran away as fast as his legs would carry him... but they followed him, yapping and yelping... Poor Actaeon! This is your punishment for being curious and watching a goddess uncovered! Fortunately, the countess was not as cruel as Diana, and had no desire to hunt him down like a stag. Upon recognising the fugitive, she too was startled, and called as loudly as she could to her hounds. The dogs obeyed her and allowed him to flee to safety behind a nearby hill. There, he collapsed exhausted onto the ground. With difficulty he managed to catch his breath, and an hour later he returned to his clothes in a despondent mood. Noticing that a rose had been pinned to his cap, though, he cheered up... 'Mama is not angry with me!' he thought. So, he dressed and went to see her... He did blush, however, when he set eyes on Emilia, and she made as if to smile, but blushed too. Tears streamed from his eyes.... The countess gave him her hand, and when he had kissed it with a particular warmth, she gently clipped his ear with the other hand. All that day, Leon seemed more sensitive, while the countess was more affectionate, kind-hearted and lovely than usual. Could she really be afraid of innocent curiosity?

(This story was never continued)

Actaeon's Odyssey on Ilkley Moor
by Helen Hagon

(A Yorkshire retelling of the story of Actaeon and Diana, based on Henry Thomas Riley's translation of Ovid's *Metamorphoses*, book III.)

There were this mountain, tha' knows, where a young lad called Actaeon 'ad been hunting wi' 'is mates. By t'middle of t'day, though, it were reight 'ot and they were proper tired, so 'e says to 'is mates: 'That'll do for now, lads. Let's call it a day, and we'll give it another go int' morning. Put yer stuff away and get thissens forty winks.'

Just round t' corner, there were a valley with this nice little spot wi' a bit of a stream that were dead pretty. Diana used to like going there ter wash off t' muck after she'd been 'unting.

Any road, she were there that day with them nymphs she allus hung out wi. She give 'em all 'er spears and arrows and that, and they give 'er an 'and tekkin off 'er clothes and sandals, like. One of 'em tied 'er hair up in a bobble an all. Then she stood int' stream and t' nymphs filled these whopping great pots wi' watter and chucked it ovver 'er.

This Actaeon chap just 'appened to be sauntering past while they were at it. It weren't 'is fault, though: 'ow the heck were 'e supposed to know they'd be there? When t' nymphs clapped eyes on 'im they didn't 'alf kick off. They were screaming their 'eads off 'cos this bloke 'ad seen 'em wi' nowt on, and they crowded round Diana to try an' hide 'er. Trouble was she were right tall and stuck out ovver t' top. She lobbed a load of watter at 'im and said: 'If tha thinks tha can tell folk tha's seen me starkers, tha's got another think coming!'

After that, she magicked antlers onto 'is 'ead, and give 'im pointy ears, and hoofs and all that, to make 'im look like a stag. Poor lad run off, but were a bit surprised at 'ow fast 'e could run. When 'e saw 'is reflection in a stream, 'e tried to yell summat to 'is friends, but all that come out were a funny groan.

While 'e were standing there wondering what the heck 'e should do next, 'e 'eard dogs barking, and it dawned on 'im that 'is own whippets were comin' after 'im. Nipper and Snapper were in t' lead, wi' Mardy Lad and Thruppence close behind. Then there were Bobby Dazzler, Crackpot, Chip Butty, Cakeole, Clartears, Jammy Dodger, Lugole, Donny Boy and Little Tyke, wi' Yorkshire Pudding and Owd Codger at back. He 'ad another go at saying summat, but nowt come out. If he hung abart there 'ed be ripped to shreds!

So, 'e legged it ovver t' moor as fast as 'e could, but them whippets run like t' clappers and caught up wi' 'im faster than tha' could say Jack Robinson. Safe to say, there weren't much left of 'im a few moments later. Diana were well chuffed when she 'eard 'ed snuffed it!

Glossary

tha	*you*
reight	*very*
thissen	*yourself*
forty winks	*a nap*
dead	*very*
allus	*always*
bobble	*hair band*
whopping	*huge*
nowt	*nothing*
lobbed	*threw*
starkers	*naked*
summat	*something*
to leg it	*to run fast*

to run like the clappers	*to run fast*
chuffed	*pleased*
snuffed it	*died*

Most apostrophes indicate a missing 't' or 'h', for example:

'e	*he*
'is	*his*
'ad	*had*
wi'	*with*

Forgive Me
by Nikolai Mikhailovich Karamzin

Who could love with so much passion
as I have loved you with all my heart?
Yet I sighed to the point of exhaustion:
in vain have I torn myself apart!

Oh, the agony of becoming enthralled,
alone, yet overcome with ardour!
It is not possible that anyone at all
can simply fall in love to order.

I have neither glory nor acclaim:
how could I ever hope to impress?
I can neither amuse nor entertain:
what grounds for love do I possess?

A feeling or a simple heart
in this world are as nothing.
What is needed here is art:
alas, in this I was lacking!

(The art of airs and affectation,
the art of artfulness itself,
the art of charming, sweet persuasion,
of seeming smarter than everyone else.)

But then I had no inkling of this:
by my love I was rendered blind.

Thus boldly did I dare to wish
that your love I may also find!

So it was: I wept, you laughed,
you mocked me for amusement's sake.
You played with me and cruelly scoffed
at the onset of my heartache!

That ray of hope and aspiration
is now beginning to fade and decline…
Another is already in possession
of your hand for all time!

May happiness and peace ever be yours,
and may your heart be filled with cheer.
Whatever destiny may have in store,
always be kind to the one you hold dear!

In the dense, dark forest of the years,
my way through life will I wend,
shedding streams of bitter tears
and – forgive me – wishing for the end!

Epilogue

An Ode to Lost Innocence

by Helen Hagon

Young Eugene and his future bride
truly were innocence personified.
Though for years he travelled far,
he returned unflawed to his Julia.
And when cruel Fate at last intervened
not even death could corrupt pure Eugene.

Dearest perfect Liza embodied
all that Erast had ever wanted.
But sadly, knowing no restraint at all,
he disfigured her immaculate soul,
then abandoned his once-beloved friend
to meet alone her watery end.

On Bornholm Island, a poor, frail beauty,
to a prison was confined by duty.
Meanwhile, in Gravesend, alone and spent,
her beloved sang a pained lament.
He sang of separation, filled with anguish,
forever from his Lila banished.

That promising child, little Leon,
always excelled and could do no wrong,
until his intentions were misconstrued
and by barking hounds he was pursued.
By Destiny herself he was corrupted,
leaving his childhood interrupted.

But corruption is of this mortal place,
while innocence is a heavenly grace.
Thus may we hope that, on the other side,
Eugene with Julia now abides,
happy Liza is reconciled with Erast,
the Gravesend stranger has his Lila at last,
and Leon's conscience is again clear,
its ugly burden having disappeared.

Bibliography

The following texts were very helpful to me while working on this project:

Karamzin, N. *Byednaya Liza*. Moscow, Russkii Yazyk, 1988. *Given to me as a present from a fellow student while I was studying in Russia a long time ago, this was the book that started it all.*

Karamzin, N., Battersby Elrington, J. Tr. *Poor Liza and other tales*. Great Steppe Press, 2019. *Four of Karamzin's sentimental tales, translated by John Battersby Elrington, a contemporary of Karamzin.*

Cornwell, N. ed., *The Routledge Companion to Russian Literature*. London, Routledge, 2001. *A collection of essays by different scholars which tells the story of the development of Russian literature.*

Hammarberg, G., *From the Idyll to the Novel: Karamzin's Sentimentalist Prose*. Cambridge, Cambridge University Press, 1991. *A thorough academic study which puts Karamzin's writing into context, and which introduced me to some of his influences, sending me hurtling down a literary rabbit hole.*

Cardiff Corvey, *Reading the Romantic Text*, Issue 12, Summer 2004: Centre for Editorial and Intertextual Research, Cardiff University. *This interesting article suggests that the identity of Karamzin's English translator, John Battersby Elrington, is not known for certain. It is possible that he was really Andreas Andersen Feldborg, a Danish author and teacher of English, and he may have produced his English translation of Karamzin's stories from an existing German one, rather than directly from the Russian.*

Karamzin on the internet

Apart from the occasional scanned copy of Battersby Elrington's nineteenth-century translation of *Poor Liza*, I struggled to find any other English translations of Karamzin's stories on the internet. However, Russian language versions of most of his work can be found at www.lib.ru and some of his poetry is available on: www.culture.ru.

Acknowledgements

Although the process of creating this book mainly involved sitting alone in a room with a computer, there are many people without whom it could not have happened. I am hugely grateful to Natasha, who gave me a copy of 'Poor Liza' on my 19th birthday in Obninsk, Russia, thus setting the ball rolling. Many thanks to my numerous Russian teachers in Bradford, Nottingham and Moscow for nurturing my love of the language. Thank you to Elena for scanning the manuscript with her keen eyes and supplying words of encouragement. Above all, I owe an enormous debt of gratitude to my patient and supportive family for letting me indulge my whim and not minding the burnt dinners too much.

About the translator

Originally from Yorkshire, Helen now lives in Lincolnshire in the heart of the UK. In addition to a degree in Russian and French, she holds an MA in Translation Studies as well as a Postgraduate Certificate in Education. She has worked for several decades with languages as a teacher, administrator and literary translator, as well as writing poetry, short stories and educational materials. In 2023 Helen set up Written Words, an online collection of resources to help writers who would like to add a little more style and flair to their work, or anyone who is simply curious to know more about the English language and its literature, including translated literature. When she is not at her desk tinkering with words and polishing texts, Helen can usually be found playing the violin and piano or enjoying the outdoors.

For more information about Written Words, visit:

Website: writtenwords.uk

YouTube: @writtenwordsschoolofenglish

Facebook: Written Words School of English

Printed in Great Britain
by Amazon